Womb Of The Morning

Cherish Him In the Journey!
Jesus, my Savior & Lord!
You are so beautiful.

Womb Of The Morning

Dearest Patricia McKiernan,
God has gifted you
with great talent
to share in His
Kingdom.
Trust Him to see
you through.
Love, Dr. Glennie P. Metz
4/28/11

Glennie P. Metz, Ph.D., R.N.

Library of Congress Control Number:		2010913905
ISBN:	Hardcover	978-1-4535-7922-0
	Softcover	978-1-4535-7921-3
	Ebook	978-1-4535-7923-7

To order additional copies of this book, contact:
Xlibris Corporation
1-888-795-4274
www.Xlibris.com
Orders@Xlibris.com
77082

CONTENTS

Dedication

To My
Wonderful Lord and Savior Jesus Christ
Who continues to help me mount up and walk in Godliness

and

To my loving husband, the godly father of our sons,
and my best friend
John
Our Fifty years together
has been a living example of
the sacrificial love and servanthood of Christ

and

In memory of my deceased parents
Oliver and **Albertha Williams**
who, under God, gave me my being to know
the importance and power of the truth

ABOUT THE AUTHOR

Dr. Glennie Metz holds a MS and Ph.D. in Counseling Psychology. She is State certified as a Psychiatric and Obstetrics / Gynecology Nurse Practitioner. Dr. Metz is also an assistant to her pastor spouse at the Refuge Apostolic Church of Christ in Deer Park, New York; Christian Psychologist, and was an adult learner at the LaSalle and Stony Brook Universities, Hunter College, Bronx Community College, and Julia Richman High School, Junior High School 159, and Public School 103 in Harlem New York all which represents the culmination of her Christian and academic achievements.

Other professional accomplishments included that of Associate Professor in the School of Medicine and Nursing at the Stony Brook University in New York, and a busy practice as a Nurse Practitioner in Women's Health for more than 30 years. For more than 50 years she has made significant contributions to the promotion of health and wellness to God's creation providing psychological and reproductive health care to minority and other populations as her calling from God. Her travel to South Africa as a researcher, lecturer and health care provider reinforced her resolve to spread the "Good News" of Jesus Christ; in conjunction with health education, spiritual guidance and support at every opportunity afforded to her.

For five years she actualized her vision in assisting and empowering women to be all that God called them to be through her oversight of, and director of "Touching Tomorrow's World" a monthly group meeting where women came together and supported each other during rough times in their lives.

For 50 years Dr. Metz has made tremendous contributions to her profession as a nurse. She completed her Doctoral Studies at the LaSalle University and was awarded a Ph.D. in Theocentric Psychology. She recently completed a two year course of study at Christian Writers Guild as a Christian writer; and is completing her first of a series of books titled *Womb of the Morning*. She maintains active membership in the New York State Coalition of Nurse Practitioners Association of Long Island, Marriage and Family Counseling, Association of Women's Health, Obstetrics and Neonatal Nursing, and has served as a member of the Nurses Advisory Council to Suffolk County Executive Steve Levy.

More importantly, Dr. Metz has been married to Pastor/Elder John Metz for 50 years. Their partnership in ministry supports her position as his assistant and Spiritual Mother to the congregation at the Refuge Apostolic Church of Christ in Deer Park, New York. She received the Gift of The Holy Ghost/Spirit, many call the second blessing, at the Greater Refuge Temple Church in New York City thirty-four years ago; joint parented two sons, David and Marcus, and supported in grand-parenting five grandchildren: Raymond, Andrew, Michael, Aaron and little Miss Avery Metz. Each of them provides her with great blessings and achievements.

Her primary goal in life is to be all that she is designed by God to be. To that end, she expects to carry the message of God's Salvation through her writings, travels, seminars, lectures and practice.

Her motto for life is—"Just do the right thing after exiting the *Womb Of The Morning*."

ACKNOWLEDGMENTS

Birthing *Womb of the Morning* was an extremely painful, yet delightful experience for me. I would first like to thank God for knitting me together in my mother's womb; breathing into me the breath of life, and for giving me the strength to see this first of five projects through to its completion.

In memory of my parents, Oliver and Albertha Williams who in vision, saw me on a specific journey and gave me roots from which to draw strength for living, loving and giving of myself to others. In memory of my siblings, Shirley Williams, Bertha Robinson, and Randolph Williams we had such fun together before tragedy hit, and you left me too soon. In memory of Grandparents Leuvenia and Moley Ellison, Aunt Lillie Mae Larkin, Ernest Ellison, Darain Keith Metz, Mother Rachel Metz, Mother Viola Williams, Mother Cora Roundtree, thanks for being part of that great cloud of witnesses, and the great role models that you were for me.

I would like to thank my patient, faithful and loving spouse, John Metz for loving me unconditionally during those times when stress was high and patience low.

To my sons, David Anthony and Marcus Raymond Metz, you showed me respect, patience and support during the many years that I spent as an adult learner.

To my grandchildren Raymond, Andrew, Michael, Aaron and Avery, your blood flows freely with love in my veins and peace in my heart for each of you. Thank you, Evath and Ursula Metz for parenting my grandchildren the Bible way, and for being godly examples to them. To my sister Gloria Pearson and my brother Glen Williams, my nieces, great nieces and nephews, I love each of you so very much. Aurelia and William my life is richer because of you and your contributions that led to the writing of this book. Pastors James and Barbara Metz your prayerful support has been a driving force in my life. Leola and James Fields, Ruby Ellison your faith in me was always evident

Having ideas is one thing. Articulating them into print is another. I am most grateful to Susan and Jeffrey Burgazzoli for their hours of proof reading and editing my manuscript. Laverne O'Reilly, Daria Cooper and Karen Herring you added to this manuscript in more ways than I can count. Also, I express appreciation to Rubi Hightower Mason for your innate ability to encourage me to stay on point when I felt like giving up the project.

To all who have believed in me and given me an opportunity, a pat on the back, a shove in the right direction, propelled me with prayers and encouragement or financial support, I say thank you, and may the Lord richly bless you for being a blessing to me. God bless you all. I love you dearly, and I mean it.

INTRODUCTION

WOMB OF THE MORNING

Come with me on a journey that every living being created by the only Wise God has traveled. The vehicle for travel on this trip; by God's design is, and has always been, the woman's womb. Before we were formed in our mother's womb God had a plan. His plan included a specific day and time for our conception, birth, life and death. However, between these events He gave us opportunities to the greatest investment we could ever make: Life's plan that began in the womb. We were equipped with every tool needed to fulfill His divine plan in and through us.

> "Before I formed you in the belly I knew thee; and before thou camest forth out of the womb I sanctified thee, and I ordained "thee . . ." (Jeremiah 1:5).

> ". . . the Lord that made thee, and formed thee from the womb . . ." (Isaiah 44:2).

We were born babies. Prior to that great day of our birth we lived life within a life. Our Mama was the custodian of the physical as well as the spiritual components of our prenatal (preborn) state of being. Of course all of this intrauterine (womb) growth and development was under God's all Seeing Eye for nine months. To a certain degree Mama determined the kind of life we chose to live, her womb was the instrument of life and not the creator of life: God is the ultimate source of human life.

> ". . . and breathed into his nostrils the breath of life; and man became a living soul" (Genesis 2:7).

> ". . . seeing he giveth to all life, and breath . . ." (Acts 17:25).

In *Womb Of The Morning* you will be drawn into the world of a fetus (baby in the womb-uterus) as she develops and matures through out her gestational (Inside womb) period. She speaks her story from inside her Mama's body as internal and external influences impact her total self. She peacefully, and without incident floats around in her fluid -filled protective bubble from the external world for a pre-assigned period of time. These formative weeks are critical in fashioning her and the journey she will travel throughout her life. The stage is set for the realization of her goals that the Sovereign One imprinted onto the essence of who she is.

In this first publication I present to you, the reader, what I believe portrays a family during faith filled times where a mother's faith, and indescribable strength, supported by the secret weapon of her soul allows her to soar like an eagle in the midst of thick and dark clouds.

The Journey begins when a teenage married couple conceives their first child while living in rural Alabama in 1942. You will be drawn into the womb-world and sense contact with a baby yet to be born as she undergoes three stages of God's workmanship in the womb: zygote, embryo and fetus. God's purpose is being carried out in each of these stages of life in the womb.

Mama's Womb of the Morning is already primed to introduce its content (baby) to the adolescent parents and the world. Morning represents new opportunities; freshness, liveliness, and the best form and frame to perform the work of the day: laboring for the prized gift from God. Primary concerns of the birthday are to seek God's presence and blessings on a most precious first event that will never be repeated. Number one is always followed by the number two.

I invite you to explore this view of life with me through the first of a series of books that will follow this special child through her wondrous beginnings and unfolding life experiences that challenges her God ordained purpose in life. Before and after her conversion experience she will fail and succeed in her Christian, personal, family, educational and professional life. Eventually she will come to realize that God's love is really unconditional; and that He is a very present help before, during and after trouble.

So I offer this book, not as a means for being a better mother, father, sister or brother, but as a new way of looking at life through the eyes of a disenfranchised baby girl born out of the womb of the morning.

CHAPTER I

Living with Life Within

Who are you wearing? This question is frequently posed by television announcers who ask celebrities what famous designer gowns or jewelry they are wearing on special occasions. Well, this is my special occasion; and yes, I am wearing a designer muumuu made by my Mama, Eartha: the most famous and influential designer in my fluid-filled world. As to jewelry, the Sovereign Designer of all creation uniquely designed my internal and external body parts. I recall hearing Mama's preacher say that God knew me before I was formed in her womb, and that He consecrated (set apart) me while in the womb to do a good work for Him. My Designer—of all that is visible and invisible—(in my confined quarters), fashioned each cell in my body (my jewelry) according to His good pleasure. To the natural eye, I am invisible, but my Designer knows me and sees me at all times.

Speak From the Womb

Mama cannot see me or touch my skin, but she is acutely aware of my living presence each time I kick her ribs, and elbow her diaphragm, and other internal structures. When I hiccough for more than a few seconds at a time, she places Papa's big, rough hands on her belly allowing him to feel my rhythmic, knocking movements. You should see the highly expressive smile on his face when we make contact with each other, albeit through skin, muscles and a big bag of water. His excitement heightens all the more when I decide to roll from side to side, and Mama's belly looks like some foreign object from outer space is rolling under her skin. He watches this action in amazement as Mama grunts in pain. For thirty-eight weeks, the Omnipotent One, (The Designer), made provisions for me to be covered, hidden, and protected from the outside world in one of His Designer's best (Mama's womb). Her progressively enlarging womb is a perfect hiding place for me until that great day: My birthday.

Poor and Pregnant

I have been wearing Mama's womb for the past thirty-eight weeks, floating around in her since late February hidden under her designer muumuu. Her designer muumuu was made from four patterned flour sacks that once contained 50 pounds of white flour (frequently used as staple food). She uses it to make biscuits; dumplings, cakes, pie crusts, gravy, and to coat chicken, pork, and beef for frying. Mama and Papa really enjoy eating crispy fried meats. I see her sitting patiently removing the seams of four similar sacks, and patterning them into a tank dress or muumuu that will accommodate her, and my growing body. She uses her creative skills in hiding Pillsbury's Best, Mother's Best Milled, and Gold Medal flour labels (blue stamp on the sacks) out of sight by sewing them in the garment's pockets, hems or seams.

Sometimes, she has to hide them with a decorative bow or scarf. These labels are not proudly displayed for the world to see. It is even embarrassing for me to share her secrets.

worldly clothes labels

Designer Clothes

Her practice as a self-made seamstress differs significantly from that of the rich and famous of Hollywood who purchase family planning, prenatal, labor and delivery room services. Her creativity and support from family and friends offers her access to similar services that promote a healthy mother and baby outcome. Women in my community deliver their babies at home with the assistance of a lay midwife. I expect that these practices will change before I reach childbearing age. Women will be forced to give birth in

Big Momma - Grandmother

hospitals under the care of Obstetricians rather than lay midwives. They will dress in a hospital gown, be forbidden to eat, placed in a hospital bed, and hooked up to an electronic fetal monitor to keep a constant check on the unborn baby's heart activity, and the activity of the mother's womb. And, for more detailed monitoring of the laboring process (mother and baby unit) an intravenous catheter will be inserted in one of her tortuous veins, and a scalp clip placed onto the fetus' scalp. I am sure that the natural, God ordained, and physically enabled means for women to deliver babies will cease.

Our small, two-bedroom house sits diagonally across the road from Big Momma's house, and directly across the road from Aunt Sadie Mae's house. Mama and Papa are so proud of their brand new house. It is one of the most modern ones in this community, structurally that is. It will serve as the residence for my prenatal, labor, and delivery room care. Unfortunately, it does not have indoor plumbing or electricity yet. That is why Mama and Papa are working so hard to earn enough money to have these services installed. They want to make a better life for me than they experienced for the past seventeen years. This doesn't mean that their parents neglected them by any means. It's just that opportunities today are more readily available to them than it was during Big Momma's childbearing years. I frequently hear them say how they want a better life for me and my siblings. Siblings, oh no! I want to believe that I am going to be their only child, and that all of their time, love, money and interests would be for me. Oh, well, I guess that I will have to share them with other brothers and sisters. We shall see about that!

Big Momma and Aunt Sadie Mae keep a close watch on Mama to make sure that all is going well. They don't believe that she is mature enough to know what to look for or do in case something goes wrong. You see Mama and Papa have only been married for a year, and they are only 17 years old. They are still called children by the older folks in the community. In fact, age-wise they are still children. In these days, Christian couples marry at a young age, and are taught that sexual intimacy is forbidden before marriage. All they know about labor and delivery is that babies are born after experiencing severe pain, and that the pain of childbirth must happen to women because of the sin of Adam and Eve in the Garden of Eden. Knowing this to be punishment from God, they accept the laboring process without question, believing that this is what God wants for them. Sooner or later my parents will learn that the original sin of our first parents was disobedience to God's command not to eat the fruit from the Tree of Knowledge, and that marriage and sexual intimacy is a divine plan of God. According to Holy Scripture, these words apply to me even before I make my painful exit from my Mama's body and my grand entrance into my new world.

"For thou hast possessed my reins: thou hast covered me in my mother's womb. I will praise thee; for I am fearfully and wonderfully made: marvelous are thy works; and that my soul knoweth right well" (Psalms 139:13-14).

Here I am resting peacefully and comfortably in my warm, cuddly nest known as the womb and uterus (I am not doing much swimming or floating because it's tight in here) that holds my protective bubble which is full of warm fluid that buffers each one of my and Mama's moves. This warm womb also keeps my temperature stable and protects me from injury when Mama bumps into the side of the stove or the wash tubs when she uses the scrub board to hand-wash the laundry.

My fun time in this place is coming to an end faster than I can believe; but for Mama it must seem like an eternity. I know that my time to exit out of these tight quarters is near when I hear Mama complaining to Papa about how tired she is, and that she can't wait until I am born. If she would take a little time out during her busy day to rest she would not feel so exhausted when Papa gets home from work. I pay special attention to her conversation with Papa. I really do want her to be okay. I don't mean to be a bother to her. She has no idea of how much I love her and am anxiously waiting to see her beautiful face in her world.

"Honey, do you want a glass of buttermilk?" Papa says, moving quickly to the ice box to get it before Mama answers. "No baby," Mama said. "I am just a bit tired tonight." "Why don't you go and lie down, and I will be in soon." "I think that's a good idea," she whispers softly as she waddles into the bedroom.

Special Delivery

It's only eight o'clock in the evening, and I don't recall them ever going to bed this early. They usually retire for the evening after nine o'clock. It must be hard for her to walk around all day carrying an extra 33 pounds of me, and other supporting structures that keep me alive and healthy all day.

I can readily understand how Mama gained so much weight in less than a year. You see, when I initially burrowed myself in her lemon sized womb she weighed about 180 pounds. Progressively, my growing presence caused her womb (my temporary world) to grow to the size of a large orange, grapefruit, honeydew melon, and finally to its present size of a seven pound watermelon. When I reach full-term or forty weeks, signals will be sent out from my huge watermelon-size hiding place (womb) to assist in initiating labor and delivery. After I am born, she will lose all of the weight that I caused her to gain. But until then, significant changes and growth will continue to take place in my and Mama's body. There will be no growth retardation in this exceptionally precious baby. In just two more weeks, I will be moving down and out of this tight space. Tight, tight, tight! It is extremely tight in here, and I am feeling the squeeze.

Two weeks went by quickly for me, and not quick enough I am sure for Mama. I hear a melody of these words ringing in the ears of my finite mind: "Oh what a beautiful morning, oh what a beautiful day, I have a beautiful feeling that everything is going well for Mama, Papa, and me today." Why? Let me tell you why this is going to be our reality. It's a bit chilly today even though the temperature outside is 57 degrees: in my space it is a pleasant 99.6 degree Fahrenheit. (A pregnant woman's temperature is a degree or so higher than normal.) Bright sunshine makes it feel much warmer, and more cheerful than the temperature suggests. I have an attraction to light, even while I am in my hiding place because it represents life, growth and love.

In this small Alabama town, our small house sits about 50 feet back from the dirt road. Mama sweeps the front porch and yard everyday as if both are extensions of the front room (living room). Each time a car zooms by, a cloud of dust forms and settles on the porch. It then enters both windows on the front of the house, and settles on the few pieces of worn furniture that is placed against the walls in the front room. It also settles on the dinner table that's located in the center of the dining room, and four high-back, wooden chairs without seat cushions. Mama and Big Momma take pride in keeping a clean and tidy home just in case someone comes by to see how Mama and I are doing. I hear them say, "You never know when someone is going to drop in un-expectantly and that cleanliness is next to Godliness." We don't have access to a telephone, and it may take weeks to receive a letter from Auntie Lucy Bell up north (New York). I don't worry about it because I am in an uncomfortable, yet secure place for the next 24 hours or less. Tomorrow, November 19th is the day that Mama, Papa, Big Momma and others have been waiting for. It is Mama's EDD/EDC (expected date of delivery or confinement). It will be a day like she has never experienced before, and one that she will never forget. I expect that Mama and I will experience an uneventful labor and a natural birth with the assistance of Miss Effie, the family's lay midwife, because this is just the way it happens in this family. I guess the impression that I am receiving about a beautiful day rings loud and clear because it will be my "*coming out*" to meet-my-new-world day.

Unlike the practice of Obstetrical care that will be in place when I am a grown-up: Here and today my Mama, and pregnant women are delivering their babies at home surrounded by their loving and supportive families in familiar settings. These practices will significantly change before I reach childbearing age. Who knows, maybe I will be in a position to assist in delivering a few babies myself? This natural, God-appointed, physically-enabled means for women to deliver babies will change. It will be mandatory that they give birth in hospitals under the full watch of obstetricians rather than midwives. They will be required to: dress in hospital gowns and lie in hospital beds, be attached to electronic fetal monitors, ordered not to eat or drink, have intravenous needles or catheters inserted into veins in their hands or arms to provide ready access for hydration, sedation, pain relief, and to administer drugs to initiate or augment the laboring process. These things will be in place if the laboring process is not advancing according to specific guidelines (labor curve). Many will have episiotomies (a surgical incision to widen the birth outlet), and /or assisted delivery using forceps, vacuum extraction or abdominal pressure applied to the woman's pregnant abdomen by an assistant. None of these interventions are going to happen to my Mama and me because God and Midwife Effie are going to take good care of both of us just like she did Big Momma when she gave birth to my Mama.

Arrival on Time

Tomorrow morning I am going to find my way out of the womb (through the birth canal) into another world. Surely Mama will be very happy to be relieved of all the minor discomfort that I have been causing her for the past nine months. At this time, she no longer considers them to be minor because they are causing her frequent visits to the bedside commode (slop jar). She doesn't chance going to the out-house any longer to meet her physiologic needs. Her feet are so swollen that they cannot fit into her shoes, thank goodness that she likes walking around bare feet anyway. Her breasts are larger and heavier than ever causing her significant back and neck discomfort. It's not fair for her to attribute all of her breast discomfort to my presence, in that they were pendulous prior to pregnancy. Now they are twice her normal size. Her breast discomfort makes it very difficult for her to sleep on her side or back. She is not aware that, if she sleeps on her back the pressure of her heavy womb on major blood vessels interferes with fresh oxygenated blood circulation to my body, especially my brain that is being developed for a particular work. That's why I kick her so hard when she does, so that she will change her position. You see how much power I have even in my unborn state to effect change in behavior of the most important person in my world. When I exit Mama's womb (my present world), and enter into a new one, I will, by the power of my newborn voice, make known to her and others what my needs are.

The countdown is on – tick-tock, tick-tock—in less than 24 hours I will be held in my Mama's long brown, sweaty arms. She, however, is not aware that I may not come today, but she is hoping that I will. I wish that I could tell her that today is the day! You see, the only way that I can communicate with her is by my activity or lack of same. If I don't move enough, she gets worried. When I move too much, it makes her uncomfortable. Up to this point, I have been making my presence, the strength and development of my muscles and bones so very real to Mama. Other signs that I am primed for delivery are increasingly evident as the time of my grand entrance approaches. Don't get me wrong. I know that I have power, but not sufficient enough to initiate the onset of labor. The process and event were predetermined by the Omniscient One (The All Knowing

God). Although, I have been causing several manifestations that precede the onset of labor on her, I still only play a small role in the process. Biological and nervous factors play a major role in initiating labor and my expulsion from Mama's body. It's time for me to come out. It's too tight in here. The squeeze is on that's different from what I have been feeling for the past 2 weeks. I feel like someone is taking their hands and trying to flatten my hiding place. It is so very uncomfortable. It feels like the squeeze is causing my heart to beat fast for a while, then it slows down to its normal rate. With the squeeze, I feel like someone is trying to place a steel cap that is 3 sizes too small on my big head. What is going on out there? I am being and feeling a little stressed now!

After supper, on this breezy Wednesday evening, Mama and Papa are sitting in the front room listening to the only record they have; a 78-rpm recorded by a popular group called the Heavenly Gospel Singers. They play this record over and over again on an old used Victrola brand phonograph given to them as a wedding present from a church brother. If it were physiologically possible, I could sing the song, *Plenty Good Room in my Father's Kingdom* in the womb (my temporary hiding place) along with them after hearing it played so many times. They sing other Spiritual songs along with singing groups: *I'm Living Humble*, *Something on My Mind*, and *Have You Got Good Religion?* Eventually, they commit to memory the words of the songs and sing them as a duet at home and in various churches where they are well received. I am going to be a singer when I grow-up too.

I overhear their conversation as Mama sits on the straight-back chair next to Papa. She elevates her swollen feet and legs on one of the dining room chairs that are lined with her bed pillow hoping to reduce the swelling. Papa, sitting next to her, wraps his large left muscular arm around her large frame, draws her close to his chest and speaks softly to her. I can't figure out what he is saying to her, but it must be something sweet and acceptable to her because she gives him a big smile. All of a sudden she lowers her feet from the chair and grunts as if something just bit her on her back. She takes a deep breath and holds it for what seems to be a full minute: I know it was only for a few seconds. Papa quickly jumps up from his chair and stands before her with his knees applying firm pressure on hers to prevent her from sliding off the chair to the floor.

"Honey, are you okay?" "I guess so. It felt like something just took a seat low in my belly." "This is the first time I have ever felt like this, do you think it's a sign that the baby is coming?" "Maybe, let me help you to the bedroom; maybe you've just been sitting up too long." "You might be right. I didn't take a nap today because I wanted to prepare a few meals for you just in case our baby decides to come tomorrow on her due date." "Let me help you undress and put on your night gown. Which one do you want?" "The pink one will be fine. Oh! Oh! Oh! There it goes again. This time I feel like my belly is pushing up against my chest. Let me just lie down now!"

"I'll go into the front room and get the other pillow and put it behind your back. It's getting dark. I will light the kerosene lamp for you." "Thanks, come and lie down next to me. I am scared!" "Let me pray for you now. God is going to see you through this and give us a beautiful baby." Papa prays a powerful prayer to God as he places his right hand on her clammy forehead:

"Father God, I thank you for my wife and the baby that is on the way. Please bring both of them safely through their valley of death called labor and delivery. Lord, you said in your Word that if I walk uprightly before you, that you would give me the desires of my heart. Now Lord, my heart's desire is to have both my wife Eartha and baby whole and well. I am thanking you in advance for the answer to my prayer request. Amen."

It is pitch black out here in the country. Only the light of the moon and the stars break the total darkness. Without electricity available to us, there is nothing to light either homes or the streets. Consequently, the majority of the community retires for the night as soon as it is dark outside. This works to their benefit since most of them get up before sunrise, which is about five o'clock during the week to prepare for work. Our local Midwife Effie, who assisted Big Momma's, and now my Mama's delivery, does not have the luxury of working by the clock as most of the community residents. She can be called upon anytime day or night, summer, winter, spring or fall, sunshine and rain to assist in the birth experience of her patients. Whenever she is needed, the family, neighbor or friend of the expectant woman will find her one way or another. They make themselves available at all times to be called upon: even to be awakened in the middle of the night to help a neighbor. The noise of an old truck in need of a tune-up is the community alarm which indicates that someone is sick or about to have a baby. It wakes up the whole community.

Outside, the dark of this night is so thick that it can be cut with a knife. Slits of light can be seen at the borders of the window of the small bedroom where the burlap shade doesn't quite fit the inner frame of the window. Flickers of light from the kerosene lamp on the bureau against the wall can be seen from the road. The visible plane of light from the window of a home at two o'clock in the morning in this quiet area of the country indicates that something very special or very sad is happening in that particular home.

> *This Thursday morning, the 323rd day of the year will be like none other in the Marcus family: I am going to make sure of that when I exit my dark, warm protective womb and make my grand entrance into their world. A world where I will bring pain, joy and sorrow to two inexperienced young people who have no idea of the struggles they are to encounter as teenage parents, others will too. Challenges and struggles will bring them to a state of maturity that they can't even imagine at this time in their lives.*
>
> *Thousands of special deliveries like mine are occurring worldwide on this November 19, 1942. Up North, three Caucasian mothers of the day, on the opposite side of the track, are preparing for the entrance of their boy bundles of joy into their new world: Franklin Roosevelt in New Hyde Park, New York; Calvin Klein in the Bronx, New York; and Gary Ackerman in Brooklyn, New York. Undoubtedly, their mothers are delivering them with the assistance of notable Obstetricians, Pediatricians and Professional Nurses instead of a Lay Midwife.*

Is it a boy or a girl? Mama and Papa will receive an answer to this special question on this great day. I have no clue of what it means to be male or female, I just know that it is getting very tight in here, and I am ready to come out. The pressure of each contraction causes my heart to beat faster. After each tight squeeze, I relax for a few minutes and almost immediately here comes another one. Midwife

Effie applies the pressure of her fetoscope on my back after each squeeze to hear if my heart rate returns to normal after the tight and long squeeze: It does, each time. As soon as I recover from the last squeeze here comes another one. How much longer before that final squeeze and powerful push of expulsion will take place? Unaware of my gender, mother is about to deliver her first baby girl with purpose.

Midwife Effie guides my head gently through the birth canal as mother screams to the top of her lungs. The room seems to shudder with each scream.

"Eartha, stop screaming and push." "I can't, I can't, and it hurts so badly." "Yes you can, listen to me, take a deep breath, hold it and push as hard as you can!" "Okay, okay, I can do it, I can do it" "That's good, that's good. Hold it, hold it." "Here he comes, here he comes."

All of us babies are "he's" until we are born and our gender is established. All of a sudden my Mama gives her final grand push to life, and I introduce myself to the outer world with a loud baby cry after twenty-four hours of hard labor.

Big Momma and Papa are waiting anxiously in the adjoining room listening for my beautiful sound of life. Once they hear my cry they will know that all is well. Here I am world, ready or not! "It's a girl. It's a girl," Effie says with joy, as she removes fluid from my nose and mouth. Papa rushes into the room as soon as I beckon for him with my cry; he didn't wait for the call to come to see his pride and joy. He stands at a distance from the bed that is covered with thick brown plastic sheets. He looks around and down at the bucket at the foot of the bed and starts to breathe fast and sweat. But, he gains his composure and goes to the head of the bed and kisses Mama on her clammy forehead. "Is she all right?" Mama asks. "She's fine, beautiful and has all of her parts." "Can I see her?" Mama says, as she focuses her eyes between her shaking legs, in the area of my cry.

Effie dries me off, wraps me in a warm blanket that she took out of the oven and places me in Mama's warm, waiting arms for my first meal at her breasts. My first breastfeeding experience is a gentle way to transition me to my new world out of the womb, and to support its contractility.

"I am going to stay with you for a few hours to make sure that all goes well."

"Thank you." "Do you want to see Big Momma now?" "Yes I do." She never took her eyes off me while talking to her. Mama kisses me on my forehead and begins to cry as Papa wraps his arms around both of us. Big Momma waits outside the room until Effie asks her to come see her new grandchild. "Praise God everything is good," Big Momma says. "Yes, Big Momma," Mama says as she closes her tired puffy, blood shot eyes. She broke a few capillaries in her eyes by pushing so hard to get me out. "Let me take the baby from you."

Big Momma takes me from her and Papa's arms, sits in the rocking chair in the corner of the room and begins to sing to me. I hear her singing a beautiful song, and pray an initial post delivery prayer for me. With tears dropping from her pretty brown eyes, she sings and prays for me.

"Jesus loves me this I know, for the Bible tells me so, little ones to Him belong, they are weak but He is strong." "Father God, I thank you for bringing us a healthy baby girl, my granddaughter. Please continue to bless and strengthen her beautiful small body. Help her to grow in the stature and admonition of your love. Protect her from all hurt, harm and danger, and help her to prosper in all of her endeavors. Teach her to love you in her youth, and to be a witness of your love all the days of her life. I thank you, in Jesus name for answering my humble request."

CHAPTER II

Dresser Drawer Bassinette

I fall into a quiet sleep and Big Momma places me in the bureau drawer, where I will sleep. This is my bassinette until I am big enough to sleep in my crib. She tucks me in and goes over to see how Mama is doing. She is sleepy, exhausted, and not aware that Big Momma is standing over her as she places her right hand on her head and begins to pray for her too. She loves to pray for people.

"Father, I thank you for my daughter and our new baby. Please bless her and Ernest Lee to be Godly parents for her. Heal her body and protect her from any infection. I thank you, in Jesus name."

Post—delivery infection is a major concern in my town. Over the past few months, I heard Mama telling Papa about how Ms. Lessie died when her baby girl was just 4 weeks old. Rumor is that she had a fever that could not be broken. Big Momma will not let that happen to my Mama, her daughter. She will pray until she sees that everything is well with Mama and me. After she prays, she goes into the kitchen to prepare supper for my family and Effie. Papa and Effie stay in the bedroom, my labor and delivery room, and watch over us. Between checking on me and Mama she sits on a dining room chair next to the bed and writes my vital statistics on a blank sheet of paper. All pertinent information about my Mama and Papa that will appear on the birth certificate must be collected now. After writing down information that includes their full name, address, color, place of birth and occupation, she asks them for my name. Since they had not decided on a name for me yet, that part of the form is left blank and instructions are given for them to decide within the next few days and get the information to her. The paper work for the certificate of birth will not be submitted until I am given a name. It puzzles me that I, a living creature, do not have a name. It even sounds funny to me.

The cuckoo clock on the plasterboard wall signals that it is eleven o'clock. It has been two and a half hours since Mama delivered me, her healthy nine-pound baby girl. Effie, with Big Momma's help, gave Mama a soothing bed bath and a relaxing back rub as Papa kept an eye on supper that was cooking on the stove. I see Mama lying there on the freshly made full-size bed covered with a new set of rose patterned white sheets that were a wedding gift from Big Momma. She is sound asleep and snoring so loud that she can be heard throughout the house. Labor and delivery was hard work for both of us, and she is finally able to rest. Her snoring doesn't bother me because I spent the last seven months hearing it as a soothing sound: just like the beating of her heart. One might call it noise, but it is like music to my ears, it lets me know that she is so very near. While she is sleeping, God is working healing miracles in both of our bodies. Transitioning from my protective home in Mama's womb to a new way of living is the handiwork of God and God alone. Of course, He uses the hands and skills of people working together with Him to accomplish a desired end: In my case a new beginning to achieve an expected end. I am living proof of the Word of God that reaffirms how I was covered in my mother's womb, and that I am fearfully and wonderfully made.

Immediately, when my wet body comes in contact with the ambient air, great changes are initiated in me. Once my umbilical cord is cut, my placenta (mother's cake) became useless, and all of my body functions are initiated in my own organs. New circulatory pathways are open and my own lungs start to acquire oxygen without which I can't live. Impact of the relatively cool air on my moist bronze skin stimulates me to breathe. Of course, I don't breathe until Effie clears away thick mucus from my nostrils. My cry, from the depth of my being, informs everyone within hearing distance that I am here, alive and kicking. No spanking for me, not now, and hopefully very few of them in the future.

Major changes are taking place in Mama's body too; that's why she needs her rest. After she rests for a while, I am put to her breast for a few minutes to develop my sucking reflex, and to determine if I can swallow liquids normally. For the first two days, her pre-milk (colostrum) is my special diet. She continues to take care of me by feeding me her pre-milk that is thicker than transitional and mature milk with all of its life advancing properties. After three days, she introduces me to true milk that will be a part of my steady diet for the next two, three or more years.

Stay out of the kitchen! Customarily, new mothers are not allowed to cook or serve food during the first six weeks after delivery. Many southern families believe that a new mother is unclean and should not prepare meals for herself or the family until the baby is six weeks old and her postpartum bleeding has ceased. All Mama has to do is take care of me and my personal needs. Big Momma makes sure that she and Papa are well fed; the house is clean, and that I get all the attention, and more, that is necessary for me to grow up healthy.

It is really good that our 10 by 12 foot bedroom is located on the north side of the house since we don't have electricity yet. This location allows the greatest source of sunlight to filter into the room during the day. Splintered, unfinished, dull light brown plank floors lay bare and chilly this time of the year. Sunlight takes the chill off the air and the floor. I don't like feeling cold, neither does Mama. Sometimes she wears socks to keep her size 11 wide width feet warm, and to avoid getting splinters in them. She doesn't need complications from an infection to impinge on us bonding with each other.

It's four o'clock in the morning, and it is pitch black outside. Almost eerie, however, since my parents gave themselves to the Lord, they no longer hold to superstitions that ghosts and witches are actively doing their evil work during their night watch. At one time in their lives, they thought that when a person sleeps, witches ride their backs causing them to toss and turn all night, and wake up in the morning feeling so tired that they cannot function well. My Papa has the best reason in the world for not sleeping so well last night. Me! He kept getting up from his pallet (couple of blankets) on the floor in the next room (my bedroom) and tipping into the room where Mama, Big Momma, and I are sleeping to watch me breathe. This is contrary to the idea that if he was out of the room, he would be able to sleep so that he could get up early and go to work. If he doesn't work, he doesn't get paid. For the past 9 months his internal alarm clock wakes him up this early in the morning, and he follows his routine of re-kindling the fire in the pot-bellied iron stove that sits in the middle of our small bedroom before he leaves for work. He is such an expert at getting the fire up and running full force again: it catches on in less than five minutes every time. In no time at all, heat radiates from the stove bringing the November temperature in the room to a comfortable level for each of us, especially me! They believe that I need the temperature of an incubator as warm as the one I was delivered of in order to be healthy and comfortable. They don't know about the brown fat that God places in my back, around my neck, in my armpits and around other organs in my body to produce heat (Thermogenesis) just in case the ambient air is too cold for me. It doesn't bother me much because I love the penetrating heat that comes from the hot pot-bellied stove. Before he leaves for work, he banks the stove so that all Big Momma has to do when she gets out of bed, where she is sleeping with Mama, is stir up the embers with the fire poke, and open the vent to get the flames up to full strength again. Mama stays in bed and leaves it only to use the bedside commode, and wash her hands in a stainless steel wash-basin that rests on a chair next to it. We both take our meals in the bedroom: She feeds me while lying in bed on her side, and Big Momma places her food on a bed tray and she eats her meal sitting up in bed while resting her back against the wall. The bed does not have a headboard attached to it.

Before coming out of the womb, I remember seeing Papa start a fire in the wood-burning kitchen stove each morning at four o'clock, and brew his eye-opening cup of coffee. Mama sits with him at the table as he leisurely has his breakfast before the truck arrives to take him to work at the steel mill. Things are different today, however. He is sitting at the table all by himself but not alone. He believes the words of a spiritual song *Never Alone*, which he and Mama frequently sing as a form of prayer. Today the words "He promised never to leave me, never to leave me alone," are ringing in his mind. When he finishes his second cup of coffee and cold baked ham and biscuit sandwich, that was left over from last night's dinner, he clears the table and leaves the kitchen.

Bring out the balloons and birthday cake, and let's celebrate my 7th day of extra-uterine life in my new world. I am adjusting very well, thank you. Now that Mama is up and about, and Big Momma doesn't spend her days and nights with us any longer we are establishing our triad routine. That is, my parents can have their first cup of coffee together in the kitchen before he leaves for work. Today we have so much to celebrate.

Papa pumps water from the pump located in the backyard about eight feet from the back porch every night before he goes to bed, and fills the 40-gallon water barrel kept in the kitchen that is never allowed to run dry. A gallon jug of cold water is kept in the icebox so that cool water is always at hand. At any time, you can find a five-gallon pot of hot water on the stove ready to use for dishwashing, hot drinks, and our daily bath. So whenever Mama has need for hot water, it is available and hot. Bath time is the highlight of my day, next to my feeding times of course.

Big Momma comes over to our house every morning to take care of us. She can walk into the house at any time of the day or night since we don't lock our doors at all. When I hear the front door open, I recognize her heavy footsteps that cause the floors to squeak upon her entrance. This time, the aroma of fresh cooked breakfast food enters the house before the sound of those heavy sole shoes that Papa gave her last Christmas. They are about a year old now and she is still wearing them every day: She loves those old worn shoes.

As she enters the house, she makes it known that she is here when she calls Mama by her pet name. "Good morning Nibs. How are two of my favorite girls doing today?" "We are good. This seventh day is so much better than the past 6 ones. She slept for four hours straight last night." "That's good. I told you that it gets better as she gets older." "Yes you did."

"Are you hungry?" "A little bit." "I brought you breakfast. I made your favorite: grits, ham, eggs and biscuits." "Thanks Big Momma, I will eat it later. I want to give her a bath first." "No, no, why don't you get up and eat something now, and I will give her a bath."

"Okay, I guess that will work best."

Big Momma takes the covered dish to the kitchen and places it on the stove. Mama raises herself up slowly from the bed and goes into the kitchen to fill her bath basin with hot water for her sponge bath. She will not be able to have the pleasure of a tub bath for another five weeks according to Effie's instructions. Both of us are living with early physical restrictions: The remnant of my umbilical cord is still attached, and I cannot be submerged in a tub of water until it falls off. She returns to the bedroom with all that she needs for her personal hygiene. I see her glance over at me as I lay still in my bassinette drawer that is resting on a table next to her bed. When Big Momma picks me up from my drawer/bassinette, she smiles and speaks sweet baby talk to me; then she takes me into the kitchen, leaving mother alone to bathe herself.

Out comes the old chipped white porcelain basin that is kept for special occasions, such as my bath by my Big Momma. Hey, this is a very special time for both of us. She takes the basin out of the trunk where all the precious and rarely used items and utensils are kept, and places it on the wooden kitchen table. She dips a tin cup into the pot of hot water on the stove and fills the basin a quarter full; then she adds enough cold water from the water barrel until it is lukewarm to the inner aspect of her wrist. It's amazing to see how she can hold me in a football hold in her left arm, and do so many other things efficiently with her right hand at the same time. The kitchen is a perfect place to bathe a 7-day old baby girl. It is always the warmest place in the house. She places a laundry basket that holds all of my toiletries and baby clothes: ivory soap, petroleum jelly, alcohol, baby oil, cotton balls, safety pins, washcloth, cloth diapers, belly bands, bonnets, under shirts, kimonos, and receiving blankets on the table. She gently lowers me from her strong and secure arms, and places me on a thick thirsty towel on the kitchen table for my sponge bath. As she undresses me and covers me with a towel she sings the lyrics from one of her favorite songs, "Lord I thank you, thank you, thank you, Lord I thank you, thank you thank you, I just thank you all the days of my life." Her melodious soprano voice is captivating and oh so soothing. I hear her repeating the words to the song over and over with occasional breaks to talk directly to me, and God.

"Baby girl, you are so beautiful and I am so happy that God brought you into my life.

You are my blessed granddaughter, and I speak health and happiness into your life. I pray that God will give you a desire to serve Him and His people in the years to come in ways that you can't even imagine. Achievement and success are yours as you follow the leading of the source of all power: God. Help her Lord to be all that she is designed by you to be."

Suddenly, I feel the touch of a soft warm cotton ball sweep from the inner to outer aspect of my eyes. She is giving me eye care, and then she washes my face with clear warm water. After that, she puts me in a football hold and washes my hair and head. My thick curly black hair is one of my assets. I say this because all my visitors make mention of my thick black curly head of hair when they visit Mama and me. I ask myself, what is my name? Up to this point I am referred to as "The Baby" or "Baby Girl". Before I complete my thought, I hear Big Momma say, as she is rinsing soap from my head: "When are these young folk going to give you a name? Soon I hope. I don't know why they couldn't come up with one before you were born. They had 9 full months to come up with a name for you, Maybe they were waiting to see you first. Okay, already, it has been one full week. Well, I am sure that whatever the name, it will suit you perfectly when they make that final decision."

She covers my head with a bonnet and proceeds to wash my chest and back without wetting my navel. She exposes only the parts of my body that are being washed at the time. She is so knowledgeable and loving. Even though she wasn't aware of the physiology of heat loss from my skin surfaces and my lack of ability to shiver, she keeps me warm. After towel drying my body she pours alcohol from the bottle onto a cotton ball and cleans around my navel: As soon as my umbilical cord falls off, I will be submerged in my bath water. I am being dressed in a brand new pink kimono; and a downy soft cloth diaper and under shirt that was dried in the noonday sun, and white booties. Now, I am ready for my breakfast. She wraps me tightly in a white receiving blanket and takes me to my Mama who is waiting to feed me before she has her breakfast. Mama's breakfast is kept warm on the kitchen stove.

Six weeks pass and I continue to cry as a means of expressing my needs to Mama. It didn't take her long to distinguish different tones and qualities of it, and to act accordingly. Sometimes she responds almost immediately when I cry, and at other times it seems like an eternity before she walks over to my crib and picks me up. Different cries are my responses to unpleasant stimuli from the environment or from within me. Either I am hungry or thirsty; cold or overheated and fatigued from crying or responding from too much stimuli from parents, family, and friends. Whatever the reason, I need fast relief from it at the time.

Mama's breast milk is my only source of nutrition that relieves my hunger pangs. Long before she decides to breast feed me, God has a plan in place for her to feed me. He speaks in His Word, early in Biblical days about the blessings of the breast and the womb.

"But thou are he that took me out of the womb: thou didst make me hope when I was upon mother's breast. I was cast upon thee from the womb: thou art my God from my mother's belly" (Psalm 22: 9-10).

Long before my conception and miraculous birth, God was preparing Mama to be the vehicle through which I am to receive essential nutrients to sustain my growth. My food (breast milk) is available to me at the right time, right temperature, and any place. She is the only one who can meet this most vital and intimate manifestation of our relationship as we communicate warmth, closeness and comfort to each other. Like the umbilical cord that sustained my vital unity with Mama in the womb: Breastfeeding unifies us outside of the womb almost as close as being in the womb did during pregnancy.

Both of us benefit from breastfeeding. There are no bottles for Mama to sterilize, no formula to buy, measure or mix, and no need for a fire in the stove to heat formula made with canned Pet or Carnation milk. It forces Mama to take time out from her busy schedule to rest, sitting or lying down, and give me her undivided attention. It is impossible for her to nurse her 12 pound baby while walking around the house and doing her chores. She has to sit down, put her feet up and relax with me every three or four hours. It also increases levels of oxytocin, a hormone that stimulates her womb to contract to minimize bleeding and to return to the non-pregnant state (size of a lemon). It may also increase the rate of her weight loss, and some protection against the early return of fertility. I want to be the only child in my family for at least four years. This may sound like I am selfish, well that's true, I am just a baby. The psychological benefits of breast-feeding: Mama's increased self-confidence and a stronger sense of connection with me are as important to me as the physical benefits. Big Momma says that, because Mama is breastfeeding me, I will be healthy, and that Mama will miss less work in the cotton field taking care of a sick baby, and spend less time and money on baby doctors. Her plans are to go back to work in a few weeks, and all the benefits of breastfeeding will last even after I am weaned.

Every few hours on demand rather than schedule, Mama meets my nutritional need as she allows me to assert a limited sense of power as a newborn. At night, nursing is easy too: No one has to stumble around the dark kitchen to find the icebox which may not be cold enough to prevent bacterial growth in milk, for a bottle and warm it as I scream to the top of my lungs. Her milk is the most natural and nutritious way to promote my optimal growth and development. There are numerous benefits of my being breast-fed: Colustrum (Mama's first milk) is a gentle, natural laxative that helped clear my intestines of its content (meconium) thus decreasing the probability of me developing jaundice. This superior nutrition from Mama's breasts will benefit me with a high intelligent quotient that will be of great value as I grow up and find my course in life. And because of our early skin-to-skin contact during breast-feeding, I will experience greater security and enhanced bonding initially to the most beautiful woman in my new world, and transpose that sense of security in my future profession. My oral muscles, facial bones, and tooth development are enhanced because I am a breast-fed baby. Also, I am less likely to be obese and have hypertension and multiple allergies. Immunoglobulin, proteins in breast milk, and especially high in colostrum, will significantly reduce my risk for bacterial, viral, and parasitic infections, and enhance the effectiveness of immunizations that will protect me against polio, tetanus and diphtheria.

CHAPTER III

Time to Go To Church

Mama prepares her and Papa's clothes for church. They call them their Sunday-go-to-meeting clothes. This is in contrast to clothes they wear to work or just around the house. I watch Mama curling her hair after straitening it with an iron comb that she heats on the hot kitchen stove. After she straightens it, she heats up a pair of iron curlers and rolls her long thick black hair between the blades until it curls to her satisfaction. After perfecting her hairdo, she dresses for today's special occasion. She sits on the side of the bed to put on her thick brown cotton stockings that are held up by twisting the top of them around the upper part of her leg and securing them in a knot below her knees. After slipping her feet into her black loafers, she slips her dress carefully over her head (new hairdo) onto her soft, round body. She looks at herself in the mirror that rests against the wall, and I hear her say, "not bad, not bad for a new mom". Yesterday, Papa bought this new dress for her from a local store over the hill. This is Mama's first new, store bought, dress since she bought her wedding dress two years ago. Her pretty dark green dress, with beige lace around its cuffs and hemline makes her look at least ten pounds thinner. She really looks pretty to me. Papa hollers out from the next room, "What did you say?" He thought that she was talking to him. She says, "Oh it's nothing". The dress is a little tight around her chest, but that doesn't bother her much because she has always been a little top-heavy.

I am the last to be dressed because I have a habit of spitting-up right after being dressed in pretty clothes. Since today is my day for coming out to meet their church family: all is to remain nice and clean. No spitting up today because my parents are going to celebrate their joy of my presence with others, and symbolically give me back to the Lord (baby dedication). They will make a public vow of commitment before the Lord and the congregation to submit me to God's will, and to parent me according to His Word and His ways.

Meet the Pastor

Mama loves God. She and Papa went to church each and every Sunday prior to the last two months of her pregnancy. Occasionally, when she got home early enough from the cotton field, she and Papa would attend Wednesday and Friday night services as well. Pastor Larkin Hunter of Zion Temple Church married them on a balmy Sunday afternoon in January 1940. Now he is going to bless all three of us, and dedicate me back to the Lord on this chilly Sunday, January 3, 1943. I think that I look like a princess today, all dressed up in my beautiful crochet white gown that covers my feet, and hides my white booties. I look good in my matching white bonnet that covers my thick, black, curly hair. The three of us could make a beautiful family portrait. Unfortunately, no pictures will be taken of this once in a lifetime event. We will just have to remember the joy and pleasure of this day: The day that I was given back to God by my parents.

Before our truck arrives at the church, we hear the congregation singing an old gospel spiritual: "Give me that old time religion, Give me that old time religion, Give me that old time religion, it's good enough for me.

It was good for my old mother, it was good for my old mother, it was good for my old mother, (and) it's good enough for me . . ."

Mama is a little nervous about today's activities. It is the first time she will stand before the congregation as a new mother. It has been about eight weeks since her last church attendance. However, many of the members visited our home two days after I was born. Pastor Hunter is the first person we see as we enter the sanctuary. He has a striking appearance: tall, handsome, dark chocolate complexion with black wavy hair that is packed so thick to his scalp with some kind of hair pomade that a wind storm could not ruffle it. He is wearing his old faithful black polyester suit that is short enough to expose half the length of his white socks that scream out from under his high-water pants. He is standing behind the wooden pulpit that he designed and built himself. He is a master carpenter who designed and built the pulpit and the lectern from which he ushers the congregation into worship, and feeds them on the Word of God. He is also the local barber. Each day of the week, except Sunday, he is working in his shop shaving and cutting men's hair. Most of his customers attend worship services at Zion Temple Church. Everyone understands that Sunday is the Lord's Day, and that no one is suppose to work—a day dedicated to the lord. That means that everyone attends church for the entire day: Sunday school, morning worship, afternoon and evening services. These services begin at nine o'clock in the morning and end with the benediction around 11 o'clock at night.

No one ever complains about the schedule: It is understood that this is God's way of life for Christians in this Alabama community. Pastor Hunter's sermon starts like a slow locomotive and ends up like a roaring train. He begins with a slow southern drawl, gets warmed up when he feels the Holy Spirit moving and becomes very animated. He walks the narrow aisle of the church proclaiming the Word of God to the hearers.

It took Mama and Papa a long time (nine months and five weeks) to come up with a name they believed suited me. One minute she wanted to name me after one of her favorite school teachers, Bonnie Jean, and the next minute she wanted to name me after a precious sister in the church, Lillimae. It really didn't matter much to Papa which name I was assigned; he was in agreement to both of them. Big Momma really liked the idea of naming me after a true woman of God, who has power with both God and man. She believed that it would be a good thing to see me and to think about this special lady every time they call my name.

My Baby Dedication event will take place after: the sermon, the altar call is made, the announcements are given, and tithes and offerings are collected. That's a long time for a baby to stay clean and wait for her memorable moments of time. However, I didn't spit up or get cranky. God was working on me even as I was waiting to be dedicated back to Him. That kind of power will affect me throughout my life even when I am walking in darkness rather than God's light.

Return the Gift to God

Pastor Hunter invites my parents to bring me to the front of the church to begin the ceremony. We face him as he faces the congregation and he gives them a charge. "The primary responsibility for the care of Lillimae, of course rests on the both of you, Brother Ernest Lee and Sister Eartha Mae Marcus. The Scriptures instruct both of you to, train up Lillimae in the way she should go, and when she is older she will not depart from it. You are commanded to bring her up in the nurture and admonition of the Lord. These commands that I give you today are to be upon your hearts, and you are to impress them on this child. Talk to her about the truths of God's Word when you are at home; when you walk along the road with her, and before you lie down at night, and when you get up in the morning."

Ernest and Eartha as you engage in this task with joy and peace, may you earnestly seek the Lord daily for His wisdom and guidance in all parenting decisions and events necessary in meeting your and her needs. For as the Apostle James says, *"If any of you lack wisdom, let him ask of God that giveth to all men liberally, and upbraideth not, and it shall be given him."* Give God thanks every day for your baby Lillimae, and for the joy and love she brings to your home and life. As she grows, may you earnestly strive to spend adequate time with her; developing a strong moral foundation for life, and an early awareness of the Lordship of Christ and His abiding presence with her.

Now, Ernest and Eartha, in the sight of God and in the presence of this great congregation, both of you have pledged to bring up Lillimae in reverential fear and admonition of our Lord; and that you will lead her to accept Jesus Christ as Savior and serve Him as her Lord as a child. In so doing, you pledge to make your home a "school" for Christian instruction.

Dedication Service

Pastor Hunter takes me from Mama's arm, and cradles me in both of his hands lifting me up before the Lord and prays a powerful prayer.

"Father God in the precious name of your Son Jesus, I give you praise for the life of this beautiful gift that you have put in the care of Ernest and Eartha for a limited period of time. Please give her a desire to love you in her youth. Protect her from diseases and infections that may affect her negatively. As she matures, help her to choose her friends wisely and to shun every appearance of evil. Bless her to be the child, young adult and woman you desire her to be in life from this day and forever more. I thank you for answering my humble prayer." After praying for me, he places me in the four arms of my parents and says the following: "In that you have dedicated your daughter Lillimae to the Lord, He now lends her back to you." Then he asks them to repeat after him the following:

"We will, by the grace of God and the guiding presence of the Holy Spirit, raise Lillimae up in the ways of the Lord as long as she is in our care."

Six Weeks Old and Partying

After church, a few members are invited to our home for dinner. We celebrate today's special events—my sixth week of life, and dedication—by over-eating and socializing with friends and family. No alcohol is served in our home nor is dancing to worldly music allowed; these behaviors are referred to as the devil's play.

Southern Cuisine

Mama didn't notice when a few of her favorite church sisters left church immediately after the dedication. They left early so that they could stop by various homes and pick up pots, bowls, and platters of collard greens, potato salad, macaroni and cheese, baked Virginia ham, fried chicken, corn bread, banana pudding and pound cake. They prepared these foods for my party last night or early this morning before Sunday school.

CHAPTER IV

The Cotton Field

Summers in Alabama are among the hottest in the United States, with high temperatures averaging over 90 °F (32 °C) throughout the summer in some parts of the state.

Large for a five-year old girl, I lay stretched out on my bed wearing a white cotton nightgown, and a stocking cap that keeps my hair in place. I know that Mama won't have time enough to comb my coarse, long reddish brown hair in the morning; I make sure that it holds every hair in place. Mama is so proud of me; she makes sure that my clothes and hair are always in perfect condition. She treats me like a precious baby-doll. Beads of sweat drip from my cute round face, (this is what everyone says about me) and my nightgown clings to my chubby frame soaked with perspiration. After tossing and turning for what seems like an eternity I finally fall into a deep sleep. Before I fall asleep, Mama peeks into my room and I hear her as she whispers to herself saying that tonight is the hottest August night in Alabama that she can remember. She releases the curtain that separates my room from hers and Papa's and prepares for bed.

The alarm clock sounds off loud enough only for Mama to hear it. She looks over at it through blurry eyes, without her spectacles. She sees that it's 5 o'clock. Hurriedly, she reaches out to silence it—almost knocking it off the bedside table with her hand—by hitting the off knob. Quietly, she gets out of bed, falls down on her knees in prayer for about two minutes. Then she makes her way to the kitchen to prime a fire in the wood-burning stove that Papa banked before he left for work two hours earlier to heat water for our personal hygiene purposes. After her sponge bath, she covers her full figured six feet tall body with an ankle-length print cotton dress, slips her feet into her old worn brogans, and readjusts her head rag before returning to the kitchen to prepare breakfast.

Our icebox stands alone directly across the room from the wood-burning stove in the kitchen. Mama takes out a slab of fat back, a bowl full of recent laid hen eggs and places them on the round wood table located in the center of the kitchen. She walks over to the tin container where bags of sugar; shortening, flour, corn meal, salt, oatmeal and grits are stored and removes ingredients to make a batch of biscuits. The smell of a hearty breakfast permeates the house, but it didn't wake me out of my deep sleep. Mama places food on the plates and walks through her bedroom to mine. Opening the curtain that separates our rooms, she looks sympathetically at me sleeping as if to say, life shouldn't have to be this way. She calls me from the door twice without any response after which she walks over to my bed and gently kisses me on the forehead. Still half asleep, I tell Mama that I am tired. She says that she understands and insists that I get up now! She asks if I can smell what she cooked for my breakfast. With that, I perk up with a resounding, yes Mama, as I sit on the edge of the bed. Mama goes back into the kitchen waiting for me to wash my face and hands for breakfast. She has my wash-basin set up in the corner of my room for me. My not moving quickly enough for Mama, she quickly gives me a sponge bath that cools me off and washes away residue from my heavy sweating last night. I dress myself and hurry out to the kitchen with a hearty appetite for my favorite breakfast. We sit at the breakfast table holding hands, as she asks God to bless the food. After breakfast, Mama washes the dishes, sets the table for the dinner meal, and prepares lunch for our meal at the cotton field. Mama can do a lot of things in the hour before the truck picks her up for work. The lunch is packed, the house is tidy, and things are in order for Mama to pick up where she left off when she gets home from work. She doesn't let anything interfere with her responsibility to her home, Papa and me.

Prepared to Work

Short hand on the clock is on number five, and the long hand is on twelve. I know that it is five o'clock and that old gray open back truck is on its way to my house.

Pick-Up Truck

There is no need for the driver to blow the horn because the engine grumbles like it has a war going on inside it. Here it comes, I hear it. Then I see black smoke sputtering from a loose tailpipe. There is so much smoke that I can't see the numbers on the license plate. It pulls up in front of my house with at least twelve people, adults and children, standing close to each other like sardines in a can. They are holding firmly to the rails along the sides of the back of the truck to keep from swaying and falling down. Two Caucasian men in the truck's cabin are talking to each other ignoring the fact that Mama and I need assistance climbing on board which is about two feet from the ground. Other laborers help us up onto the truck. I whisper into Mama's ear, holding onto her as tightly as I can. "Mama, I don't like riding back here!" "I know baby. We won't have to do this much longer." "What are we going to do?"

"We'll talk about it when we get home tonight. You'll be all right. Just hold tight to my dress baby."

After hours of the bumpiest ride in my young life, the truck pulls into the cotton field and stops abruptly such that he intentionally tries to throw us off balance. One of the task-masters opens the passenger door of the cabin and walks around to the rear of the truck like a soldier. He shouts, as if everyone is hard of hearing saying, "Move it! Move it! Let's go. Everybody out, there's a lot of cotton to be picked today." One of the laborers mumbles loud enough for Mama to hear him say: "Who does he think he's talking to? I am old enough to be his father. That young whippersnapper hasn't even gotten wet behind his ears yet!"

"Don't waste your energy man. Save it for working under that hot August sun that is waiting to shine on us this afternoon."

A Day in the Field

Mama, standing six feet tall, looks out at the sea of cotton plants that await her picking. She adjusts her straw hat over her head rag to block the sun from her eyes. Looking down at me, her hot and uncomfortable baby girl, she says, "This is the last hot summer that will find me picking cotton for 'the man'. This time next year I am going up north to make a better life for us. You just wait and see. It will happen!" Squinting, trying to protect my eyes from the sun, I ask, "Mama, what's up north; are you going to leave me? Don't leave me Mama. Can I go with you, please, please, Mama, can I go, too?" "Baby girl I make this promise; you will *not* be a cotton picker when you grow up. I want you to get a good education so that you can have a better life than this. Come on, we can't talk now!"

After attaching her burlap sack over her shoulders she walks, kneels and occasionally bends at the waist between two rows of cotton plants. She takes a firm grip on fluffy puffs of cotton and pulls them from their burrs and places them in the sack as quickly as humanly possible. She moves fast, real fast as she picks cotton from both rows at once under the watchful scrutiny of the supervisor who makes sure that everyone works diligently. Playing around at her side I pick a few bulbs and playfully put them in the sack, making a game of it.

Trauma in the Field

Under the blazing mid-day sun, Mama drags her burlap sack that grows heavier on her back as the day wears on. She works very hard trying to pick at least three hundred pounds of cotton each day. Bringing home at least 20 dollars each day makes her happy, knowing that she is helping Papa pay the bills.

Picking Cotton

The sweet sound of the twelve o'clock siren goes off. It's time for Mama to take a break, and it is just in time to keep her from having a heat stroke. Sweat pouring from her face as a dripping faucet is worrisome to me, but not to her. Her long sleeve tank dress, soaked with perspiration, clings to her full figured body.

Cheated By the Man

As soon as she hears the siren she breathes a sigh of relief, and does not pull another bulb. She drags her burlap sack, which is filled to the top, over to the weighing station. I keep a firm grip on her wet, below the knee length dress that has two pockets big enough to hold lunch for both of us. Surprisingly, she hears that her pick weighs much less than her expectation. I hope that the scale is calibrated correctly. With a sad sigh she takes the ticket from the supervisor, grabs my hand and walks over to the water barrel to get water for both of us. Well water is free and available to us by the owners. However, she has to fetch it herself from the water barrel located at the weigh station. She carriers her twelve-ounce tin cup with her everyday so that she doesn't have to drink from the community dipper. It comes in very handy out here in the field. She gives me a drink first, and then she gulps down 2 cups of tepid, yet refreshing water. Even though it is not cold, it quenches our thirst. After her last gulp she gives a sigh of relief, refills the cup and we head back to her favorite shade tree where we sit down on burned, sharp blades of coarse grass to rest a while, and eat lunch. She pulls out a greasy brown lunch bag with our sun warm biscuits and crispy fried fat back, and she says a brief prayer of thanks. We share the cup of water.

The siren signals before we take our last bite indicating that we have 5 minutes to get back to our place on the field. Half an hour is a very short time for Mama and me to eat lunch and take care of business too. Both of us are slow eaters.

I can't believe how easily Mama finds her way back to her place in the field. She is very smart. That's what I hear Papa tell her all the time. After lunch, Mama seems to work much more than she did before lunch. A new surge of energy soars through her body. I can hardly keep up with her, she moves so fast. Burrs from the cotton plants scratch her big hands and long fingers until thin streams of blood spurt onto the fluffy white cotton balls. It looks like tinted cotton candy to me. Every few minutes I see her wipe beads of sweat from her ebony face with the back of her bruised rough hands. Sweat ripples down from her forehead along the sides of her nose and cheeks. The smell of salty sweat attracts dog flies and swarms of tiny gnats that are a constant nuisance buzzing around her ears. Between picking cotton and swatting flies and gnats from her face, ears and arms I can imagine that she feels like giving up right now. Her burlap sack presses hard on her back. Every few minutes she tries to adjust it to a less irritated area on her body. Now I understand why Big Momma rubs her down with liniment some evenings after her bath. This evening, I saw the bruises on her rib cage and back from hauling that heavy cotton sack. Seeing her fight the elements, even as a 5-year old, I am able to understand that her job hurts her, causes her pain, and that she wants to find a better way to make a living for us. I believe that Mama's pocket of snuff (pulverized, smokeless tobacco) that fills her left cheek makes it look like she's holding a large jawbreaker (solid candy ball) in her mouth. The nicotine probably keeps her calm, and alleviates some of her physical and psychological pain while she works. Every now and then she spits (*brown saliva*) saliva that accumulates in her mouth around the snuff, and a shower of it splatters back into her face when a warm breeze blows our way.

Out of the Cotton Field

At the end of a ten-hour day, she drags her tired and aching body home on a truck with people who are tired and have body odor. After the truck makes at least ten stops, it finally arrives at our house. Mama and I get off the truck and rush into the house as quickly as possible and put our stuff down on the chair. It is her daily practice when she gets into the house to wash her hands then go to the ice box and pour and gulp down two tin cups of cool water. Then she collapses on the porch swing for a few minutes before starting her homework. After she rests a while, she gets off the swing, changes from her work clothes into a housedress, washes her hands again and prepares dinner. Before you know it the smell of fried pork chops permeates the house and flows over into the surrounding houses. This evening, we are also eating left-over turnip greens, sweet potato pone and cornbread from last night's meal. It doesn't take Mama long to forget about her workday in the field, and concentrate on her family. Before she went back to work, she made it clear to Papa that she would never allow her job to interfere with her responsibilities at home. Papa usually arrives home from work as a steel mill worker two hours after Mama does. This gives her enough time to tidy up the house, wash our under-clothes, and prepare dinner before he gets home. I think that she is trying to hide from him just how hard she works because she wants to keep her job, and the promise she made to him. Dusting the furniture is one of the necessary tasks she hates. She hasn't given me that job yet but I am sure she will do it soon. Since the roads are not paved, a cloud of dust rises with each passing car and settles in the house every day. Mama leaves all the screened windows and doors open all summer and fall, they are our only source of ventilation during these hot and humid days and nights. I have never seen them use a door key to enter the house; they just push it open and walk in. Neighbors watch out for, and have trust in each other.

Supper time is one of my most favorite times of the day. Mama is such a good cook, I hear Papa tell her that all the time. Papa is dropped off at the house on a big truck that makes a lot of noise as it comes down over the levy. A trail of dust follows it all the way to our house; that is why Mama has to dust the furniture so often. Before it arrives at the front of the house, I let Mama know that he is home.

"Mama, Mama, Papa is home." Mama looks back at me from the stove as she hurriedly turns the last of six pork chops that are frying on the stove. "Run to the door and open the screen." "Yes, Mama."

I lift the latch on the screen door, and as soon as I do, Papa opens it, picks me up and hugs me so tight that it almost takes my breath away. He kisses me on the cheek and lowers me to the floor, as he asks: "How is my precious one doing today?" "I am good, Papa."

He takes me by the hand and says, as he walks me into the kitchen to greet Mama, "Whatever your mother is cooking, it sure smells good." He walks over to her and gives her a quick kiss on her lips (embarrassing) as he looks over her shoulders to see what is cooking on the stove. My Papa works hard and he loves to eat. Mama is always telling him that "It's a wonder you remain so thin with all the food you eat everyday! I guess it all goes and settles in your feet." Papa has really big feet.

"Hi Sugar Baby, how yawl doing?" "Alright, I suppose, just a little tired. How was your day?" "I am just glad to be home and to know that I am off work for a couple of days."

"Me, too. Honey, after supper I need to talk with you about a revelation I received at work today." "Is everything alright there?" "I left your wash basin on the back porch, why don't you go and wash up for dinner? We will talk about it after dinner."

Papa moves quickly on his long lean legs into the bedroom to change out of his work clothes before going out to wash his hands and arms. Mama sets the table while he is preparing for supper. On the weekends, when all three of us are home together, we eat four meals . . . . breakfast, lunch, dinner and supper. It's like our days revolve around meal planning and eating southern cooked food.

Our home does not have electricity to light up our dining room yet. One day, I know that we are going to have electricity throughout our home. Kerosene lamps with chimneys (the globes that are put on them) in each room provide us with light for dining and to do what is necessary. Systematically, every evening Mama goes into each room, removes the globe from each lantern, raises the wicks ever so slightly and lights them with a stick match that is ignited after scratching it on the rough side of the match box. Often times the globes become sooty and Mama cleans them with soapy hot water so that the light will shine brighter.

Supper smells so good, and I am so hungry, but I have to wait until supper time to eat with my parents. Mama doesn't allow me to eat anything between meals; I can drink milk or water while we wait for Papa to come home from work because she says that snacking will take away my appetite. I don't think so! This is the rule in our house and I have to follow it even though I don't agree with the rule. One thing I do know, I am not to question my parents about anything that involves their childrearing practices. I am taught from an early age that to be seen and not heard unless I am given permission is the way it works in this home. Otherwise, I am doing what they call *sassing* and trying to be grown. Mama serves Papa's supper on a big plate piled high with food. His is always placed on the table first. "Big eating" is a southern hallmark, and Mama is proud to spread a large quantity of good tasting food before us. I may be sorry about this habit-forming practice in my adult life.

After serving Papa, Mama places my baby plate on the table in front of me. My pork chop is already cut into bite size pieces. I haven't learned how to use a table knife yet. Mama's meal portion is about half the size of Papa's. Tonight's supper of fried pork chops, fresh turnip greens, fresh sweet potato pone, and corn bread satisfies us as all of our meals do. Sweet tea compliments the meal for Mama and Papa. I am not allowed to drink beverages with caffeine; therefore, a tin cup of milk is placed before me tonight and at every meal. The best part of the meal for me is always dessert. I love to eat sweet foods like sweet potato pone or hoe cake; a pudding resembling a round pan of bread.

I feel Mama's tension rising as she tries to eat her supper. She sits nervously moving her food from one side of the plate to another with her fork. I believe that she is trying to figure out in her mind how she is going to tell Papa that she is going to quit her job at the cotton plant and move to New York so that we can live a better life. I remember her telling me this afternoon that, "This time next year I am going up north to make a better life for us."

Papa asks Mama, "What's the matter Sugar Baby, ain't you feeling good? You didn't put a morsel of food into your mouth yet!" He had finished his supper before Mama put any food in her mouth. He eats quickly.

"I have a lot on my mind." "Don't let it keep you from eating your supper, you need your victuals." "I know, but I just can't eat now. Maybe I will eat later, excuse me." Mama says, as if she has something stuck in her throat. She pushes her chair back from the table, gets up quickly and goes out on the front porch and sits on the swing. It's after sundown and she knows that the kerosene lamp in the house attracts all kinds of bugs to the windows and front door. I hope the bugs don't bite her.

"What's the matter with Mama?" "I don't know Precious but I will find out. You finish your dinner now, you hear?" "Yes, Papa." I wonder if he hears me as he rushes out to be with her.

"Come on and talk to me!" "Can we talk about it tomorrow? I am very tired and need to spend a little time alone with my thoughts. Will you pray with me now?" "Sure I will. Let's go inside now," he says as he extends his hands to help her off the swing. I am to remain at the table and finish my supper while they go into the front room to pray. Papa removes two cushions from the straight chairs, and drops them on the floor in front of them. They kneel on them, close their eyes and rest their folded hands on the naked seats of the chairs.

Papa starts the prayer as always and prays out loud enough for me to hear every word that he says:

"Father God in the mighty name of Jesus, I thank you for this day that you have allowed me and my family to see. I thank you for keeping us safe as we traveled the dangerous road ways to and from our jobs. I even thank you for the jobs that you allow us to have so that we can buy food, clothing and shelter. Now Lord, I know that you know what is troubling my wife. Please speak to her heart and mind, right now I pray! Deliver her from anything that's trying to steal her peace and joy; and give her your divine direction. We both believe your Word that says in Psalm 46:1-2, that you are our refuge and strength, and our very present help in all of our times of trouble. God, relieve my wife from her trouble, please. You tell us not to fear, though the earth be removed, and though mountains be cast into the sea. Help us trust you more and not be discouraged when things don't go the way we think they should in our lives. We are waiting for an answer from You. Unless we hear from You, we don't know what to do. You always will come through for us just in time. This has been proven to us so many times in the past. There is no doubt in my mind that You have already worked it out for her. Thank you Lord for answering this prayer request."

Mama remains quiet as Papa prays. However, I overhear her sobbing throughout the prayer. Papa helps her up from her knees and encourages her to reheat her supper and eat. She does just that, while he helps me prepare for bed. He places my tub of bath water in my room and tells me to call him when I am ready for him to wash my back. I sit in the tin tub that sits on the floor in the middle of my room with a secret that Papa doesn't know yet. I know that I can't talk to him about it until Mama does. In a few months I will be six years old. I overhear people say that I am older than my years. Later on, I am sure these words will make sense to me: today they do not.

"Papa, Papa, I am ready for you to wash my back." He leaves Mama at the dining table and comes to me. I give him the wash rag and he soaps it up and gently scrubs my back. It feels so good. I love having him or Mama give me a back rub; it helps me fall asleep faster. By the time I finish my bath Mama finishes her dinner. She leaves the dishes and comes into my room to finish preparing me for bed as she does every night. We always pray before she tucks me in.

Papa comes in after our time together and kisses me on my forehead and says, "I love you Precious, sweet dreams." Both of them leave my room together after she snuffs out the flame on the kerosene lamp. The smell of kerosene lingers (I don't like the smell) for a short time in the air until I fall asleep. I don't wake up until she calls me in the morning: this is because I am not allowed to drink liquids after supper.

Working together, they finish cleaning up the kitchen. When I hear the back screen door open, I know that Papa is about to dump the last of the leftovers, and dirty dish water into the slop bucket. A large, fifty-pound lard container is kept outside the kitchen door for this purpose alone. Throughout the day, small pieces of edible food used in preparing meals, leftovers, and even the dirty dishwater with lye soap residual is dumped into the slop bucket. Our pair of pigs (Boar & Sow), a wedding anniversary gift from Big Momma and Grandpa, awaits their supper with great anticipation as I do every evening. These starter pigs are a fifth wedding anniversary gift that will keep on giving for years. On occasion, I like to watch my strong Papa carry the big bucket over to the pig-pin and pour it over the fence into the feed trough. Their sucking and slurping noises fascinate me. I laugh when I see pig soup splash off their snouts and heads when they start to eat as it is coming down to them. They can't wait until Papa finishes pouring the slop into the trough before they start eating.

CHAPTER V

Saturday to Remember

Saturday is wash day in our house. Mama gets up the same time on Saturday as she does during the week, and washes the white and colored clothes separately in old dinted tin tubs placed on three planks of wood that rest side-by-side on three sawed-off tree stumps. They are an equal distance from each other outdoors along the south side of the house. She fills and hauls at least 10, 2 gallon buckets of water from the water pump to fill the iron wash-pot that is set up on a brick platform. She starts a fire under it with sticks of fire wood taken from the wood shed. When our clothes are really dirty she boils them in this pot before transferring them to a tin tub to be scrubbed on the washboard that is constructed with a rectangular wooden frame and a series of ridges for clothes to be rubbed upon. Before transferring the clothes from the hot water pot to the sudsy water tub, she agitates them using the same three feet long wooden pole that she uses to transfer the hot clothes on. Using the pole in this manner helps to loosen up some of the dirt from them. When the water temperature is safe enough for hand washing, she places the wash-board in the tub's soapy water, squeezes and rubs them with her bare hands against the ridged surfaces on the washboard to force the soapy cleansing fluid through them to carry away dirt. Papa's work clothes are really dirty and greasy and require a great deal of scrubbing to clean them. Mama applies heavy pressure on the washboard so hard that sweat pours from her face and head in the same way that I see it happening when she is working in the cotton field.

Mama is very particular about how Papa looks before he goes off to work: He also takes pride in how he looks even at work in the steel mill. She takes a bar of lye soap that she made using lye, hog lard and wood ashes a few months ago, rubs it on the garments and scrubs away. She is an expert at making it now . . . it wasn't always that way. One of her earlier batches of soap didn't turn out right and she threw it away. Mama doesn't like to waste money, she says that it does not come easy to her; therefore she has to manage it well.

Not only does Mama make her own laundry soap in the kitchen, she also makes her own laundry starch that gives our clothes a special look and feel. She cooks laundry starch on top of the stove sometimes before or while she is washing the clothes. Both of us eat small chunks of dry Argo starch before she pours it into hot water to cook until it reaches the thickness that she likes to starch Papa's shirts and my dresses. Usually, after the final rinse, Mama dips the collars and cuffs of Papa's shirts into the liquid starch and hangs them on the clothes line to dry. After they dry, she sprinkles them with fresh water, rolls them into a ball, and places them in a towel to iron later. This makes them easier to iron giving them a like-new look.

After scrubbing the clothes on the washboard, she hand-twists them and places them into the second tub which has clean cold water to rinse and twist the soap out; then to the third tub for the second rinse. She squeezes out as much water as her tired scarred hands can tolerate, and then she hangs them on a clothes line attached between two trees for them to sun and air dry. In the hot summer time, they dry within an hour or two, but in the winter time they freeze on the line and must thaw out before they dry under the warm sun; this can take a couple of days.

Most Saturday's, Mama completes the washing and ironing before night fall. However, ironing is more of a challenge for her than washing the clothes because it is hard for her to keep the iron hot long enough to get all the wrinkles out. Every few minutes the iron's heat is lost and she has to walk back and forth to the wood burning stove to reheat it. It's a good thing that she does the ironing in the kitchen close to the stove. That's why it usually takes her more than three hours to finish ironing the pile of freshly washed laundry on Saturdays. It doesn't take Big Momma that much time to finish ironing because she uses two irons instead of one. I really don't understand why Mama uses only one iron. When I get older, I am going to buy her another iron so she can do it like Big Momma. It must be okay with her because she never complains about it.

She hangs each piece of clothing on the back of the bedroom door after she irons them. When she finishes, she puts my clothes (dresses) on nails on my bedroom wall, and her and Papa's on their wall. She places all the other clothes in dresser drawers in each of our rooms. She puts away some of my clothes in the drawer that was my baby bed for a while when I was very little. Usually when Mama finishes the laundry, we either go across the road to Big Momma's for supper or we sit around the fireplace and read the Bible or listen to the radio.

An Unusual Saturday

Mama appears in the doorway of my room looking tired and wearing her Saturday morning cotton sack house dress. She calls out to me and I am in such a deep sleep that I think I am dreaming until she comes over to me and taps me on my back. I like sleeping on my abdomen ever since I was a baby. It's hard for me to get up this morning. Usually, the aroma of breakfast foods works as an alarm clock for me on Saturday mornings. As a five year old, I can tell when things are not right in the house between Mama and Papa. They usually keep their distance from each other during these times until they talk about what is bothering them. After that, everything is back to normal.

Finally I hear her say, "Wake up, baby girl, it's time for breakfast." She walks away to finish setting our plates.

I get up and go through my daily routine of washing up at the small wood table that is over against the wall that Papa made for me when I was a baby. I put on my clothes as fast as I can and rush to the kitchen table for breakfast. We eat breakfast in the kitchen and supper and dinner in the dining room.

"Sit down and eat your breakfast child! Remember to say grace." When she calls me "child" I know that she is upset about something. This time I know that she is not really upset with me, but about her moving to New York to make a better life for me and Papa. I bow my head and fold my hands together under my chin and repeat the only meal grace that I know.

"Father God, bless this food for our everlasting good. Amen." A small plate of hominy grits, fried fat back, a fried egg and a buttered biscuit is placed before me. I like sipping a tin cup of thick buttermilk with my meal.

"Mama, where is Papa?" "Papa ate already; he's doing his outside work."

"Can I go outside when I finish eating?" "Not today, baby girl, he is very busy. He has to finish early today because we are going to town this afternoon. You stay here with me. I want you to stay with Big Momma while we are gone. Okay?" "Yes Mama."

When I finish eating, I go back to my room and make my bed. Mama taught me how to do that last Saturday. I am a big girl now! After I make my bed, she comes in and tucks in the covers on the wall side of the bed. I can't reach over there yet. After we are done, I play with my toys while Mama cleans up the kitchen, and prepares today's lunch and tomorrow's dinner and supper. We usually eat dinner and supper leftovers for the following day's lunch.

Papa walks into the house all sweaty and dirty at 10 o'clock. Mama says, "Baby, why don't you go and wash up so we can get going." Papa doesn't answer her, but walks into the room to prepare for the hour long trip to town. Before you know it, he walks out wearing his church go-to-meeting pants, long sleeve white shirt, and black patent leather pointed toe shoes.

He takes a last look in the mirror after he puts some sticky stuff on his black curly hair and gives himself a pleasing smile. Walking out of the room into the kitchen I hear Mama say, "Look at my handsome husband. You are the best looking man in this town." "Oh, come on," he says. Mama walks over and kisses him lightly on his clean shaven cheek. "Baby take baby girl across the road to Big Momma's so that as soon as I am ready we can go." "Sure thing," he says, excitedly.

"Honey, are you ready yet?" "Yea, I'll be right there." "You look pretty nifty today yourself." "Thanks, but I wish that I felt as good as you think I look." "What do you mean?"

"You must have an idea of what I am going through these last few days. You must know that I have something pressing heavy on my heart." "Surely, you have not been yourself over the past week. Is it something that I said or did?" "Oh, no, no, you are a wonderful husband and I love you more than life itself. But you need to know that there is more in life that I want for us and our daughter. And I know that you want more for us too." "Honey, I know, but I am doing the best that I can at this time." "I know that baby, and I appreciate all that you do. I am sorry, but it is not enough for us to live the kind of life that I believe God wants for us." "So what do you think we can do?" "Well this is what I want to talk with you about. Last night I told you that I received a revelation while I was in the cotton field yesterday. Remember?" "Yes, I do. What was the revelation?" "Well, I decided that I am not going back to that cotton-picking job ever again!" "Woman, what in the world are you talking about? You know that I can't make it without your financial help. Oh, Lord Jesus, what are we going to do?"

"Wait a minute honey, don't get so upset. I have a plan. But, if you don't agree with it, I will not do it. One thing is for sure, I am not going to pick another bulb of cotton for another soul. If necessary, I will stay home and take in laundry for the white man and his family."

"No wife of mine is ever going to wash and iron other folk's clothes to make a living. You will not do it as long as you are my wife. You hear?" "Yes, I hear everything you say," she says in a high pitched tone, revealing her real feelings of frustration and trepidation with respect for his authority. "Stop talking now, and listen to a plan that may work well for all of us!"

"Okay, go on," he says as he stumbles over his words trying to regain his composure.

"This is my thought, and I took time to pray about it. You know that it is our practice to talk to God, and seek His direction before we make decisions about anything." "Yeah and . . ." he says sarcastically. "Listen," she catches herself before saying anything that may irritate him more. "Let's stop talking and ask God to direct this discussion. I see already that the enemy is trying to edge his way into it." "I am sorry, he confesses, I love you. I love you with all that there is in me to love a woman such as yourself. And I have learned over the past eight years of our marriage that you are a woman with high expectations, not only for yourself, but for the entire family. You are right, although we are poor, we don't have to remain in our present condition."

"Thank you for loving me, and trusting my judgment," she quivers with delight. Can we pray now?" she asks as she takes his hands and squeezes them tightly. Both of them stand holding hands in a time of quiet prayer for about 45 seconds before they walk out together to the car. Mama usually doesn't talk with Papa about things that can make him upset when he is behind the wheel of the car. She is afraid that they might end up in an accident. But today is different, she discusses her plans to move to New York; find a job there, and eventually send for Papa and me when she is settled. Mama asks Papa as they walk over to the car, "So, Ernest Lee Marcus, what do you think about me going to New York, and us starting a new life there?"

"Honey you have to understand that I am not happy with the idea, but you have to do what you feel lead in your heart to do," Papa mumbles as he opens the car door for her. "I fear for your safety, making that long train trip up north all by yourself. I know how you don't like to be put down by anybody; especially the white man. If you speak out against anything that bothers you, you may end up in jail or dead."

"Don't you worry about me," she says, looking straight ahead to keep him from seeing the tears that fill her eyes. She settles herself in the passenger seat of their old jalopy, and promises "With the help of The Lord I will be alright. You just wait and see!" "I guess there is no way that I can talk you out of it," he pleads. He remains quiet for a moment before he relates that what he's feeling now is similar to feelings he had when he was just eight years old: His father told him that he was going to Louisiana to help make a better life for him and his mom, however, it never happened! Dad didn't keep his word. He never returned for us. "Ernest, I promise to keep my vow to always love and respect you as my husband and father of our beautiful daughter. Both of you are so precious to me, and I promise never to do anything to hurt either of you."

It's been two weeks since I overheard Mama and Papa talking about Mama going up north to make a better life for us. Since then, I wake-up every night and it takes a long time for me to fall back to sleep. They even went into town to buy a one-way train ticket to New York, and new clothes for her to take with her. She usually makes her own clothes, but this time Papa took her shopping to buy whatever she needs to take with her. I saw her when she pushed the bags with her new clothes in them under her bed. I didn't let her know that I saw them. Are they going to tell me that she is going to leave me in a few days? Tomorrow I am going to be six years old, and I hope that Mama won't go away before baking my favorite cake for my birthday.

It's still dark outside as I hear Mama and Papa talking. Through sleepy and dim eyes, I see the face of my lighted clock on the dresser. The small hand of it is on four and the long one is on twelve. It takes a few seconds for me to realize that it is four o'clock. Since it is still dark outside, it has to be early morning. It is four o'clock on Saturday morning, my birthday. Mama taught me how to tell time when I was four years old. Today is a turning point in my life in more ways than I can understand. I am six years old!

CHAPTER VI

My Birthday Gift from Mama

This Saturday morning on November 19, 1948 is my big day; it's my sixth birthday and I know that I am going to have a good time with my friends who live across the road and over the levy. I just know that Mama has invited some of my Sunday school friends too. We are going to have homemade ice cream and my favorite yellow cake with chocolate icing. Mama makes the best cake in the whole wide world. Every year she and Papa make my birthday a very special one. I am not as happy today as I think I was last year on my birthday because Mama is going away. I don't want her to leave me. I love her so much because she takes good care of me. Big Momma and Papa take care of me too, but not like Mama. Sleep didn't come easy for me last night, so many thoughts rushed through my mind. Mama is leaving me, and she didn't tell me about it; and my birthday party.

I get up and go through my usual Saturday routine after Mama awakes me. This morning it takes her a long time to get me out of bed because I didn't sleep good last night. Breakfast time on Saturday is always special for all of us. This is the time that we talk about those things that are very serious. I know that some serious talk is going to take place today even if it is only about my birthday. Birthday talk is very serious to me. It means receiving new toys, clothes, ice cream, cake and playing games with my friends. Of course my friends' parents walk them over to my house and talk with Mama and Papa for a little while and then they go home. When they come to pick up my friends Mama and Big Momma usually give them some food to take home with them. In our house, Mama always cooks more food than we can eat just in case someone comes by there is enough food to share. Most of the people we know don't have a lot of food. They think that we are rich because we have a car, a relatively new house, and that both my Mama and Papa have jobs. They know that my parents are liberal givers not only to our neighbors but to the church too. They pay tithes to our church where we go every Wednesday and Friday nights and every Sunday. I overhear them say that God will take care of people when they do what He tells them to do. I want to do what God tells me to do too, because I like the way we live. My house is better than my best friend Phyllis' house: her family doesn't go to church. Maybe that is why they don't have money to buy furniture for their front room. Her house is furnished only with beds, a kitchen table, and milk crates for chairs. So I can see why she may think that we are rich because her family is poorer than mine is. She is 6 years old too, but she didn't have a birthday party either.

After papa prays over our breakfast Mama looks directly into my eyes and talks to me like I am a big girl. "Lillimae, baby, your Papa and me are so happy that God gave you to us, and we want you to know that. Today is your very special day and we want you to remember it as a turning point in your life."

"Mama, am I going to have a party today?" "Yes, baby, we went shopping a couple of weeks ago to buy your birthday gifts." "What did you get me Mama, what did you get me?"

"Do you remember when we were looking through the Sears Roebuck catalogue and you saw that pretty yellow haired doll?" "Yes, I remember, I remember, did you get it for me?"

Mama reaches under the table and pulls out a box and sets it on the table in front of her. She opens the box as she smiles from ear–to–ear, and sees a beautiful blond and blue-eyed Caucasian doll. She lovingly draws her to her chest and kisses her on her forehead.

"Mama, Mama, thank you, thank you so much. I love you Mama. She is just what I wanted. Papa, Papa, look, look, isn't she beautiful?" "She is beautiful, just like you," Papa says."

Mama and Papa sing the birthday song to me, and then each of them pick me up and give me a tight hug, and love kisses on my cheeks. Picking me up is no problem for either of them even though

I am told that I am big for my age. Mama is almost as strong as Papa is because she is taller and wider than he is.

I felt a little sad this morning because I thought that Mama was so busy working on getting ready for her trip up north that she forgot all about my birthday. And besides, she didn't tell me that she was going away. These were my thoughts up to this morning. I am really upset with Mama and Papa because they don't care about me. They give me so many love-kisses and take care of all of my needs. Yet, she is going to leave me and Papa here by ourselves as she goes up north to live a better life without us.

After we celebrate my breakfast birthday time, Mama seems to be a little sad. She takes my doll from me and places it on the table. Pulling my chair in front of hers, so that we are face-to face, she shares her plans with me. Papa just sits there without saying a word looking at both of us with a sad face too.

"Lillimae, Mama has to go away for a time, and I want you to stay with Big Momma until I send for you and Ernest Lee. You remember last summer that I said that I will not work the cotton field again." "Yes Mama, I remember." "Well, I am taking the train to New York on Thursday. I know that you don't want me to go but I have to in order to set each of us up for a better life." "But Mama, we are rich, what else do we need?" "Rich, what does it mean to be rich?" "Phyllis said that we are rich because we have lots of food, a house and a car." "Well, in a way I guess you could say that we are rich in comparison to her and her family, but Papa and me want better for you and for ourselves, and God is opening up that door for us."

"So, when you go up north will we become rich?" "We will live another kind of life. A life where you will be able to excel in whatever way you choose. I know that you are going to be great at whatever you choose to do. I want you to believe that. Look how good you do in school. You are one of the smartest students in your first grade class." "Yes, I am smart, and I want to be a teacher just like Miss Rose." "I am asking you to tell me that it's okay for me to take this trip. Papa says that it is okay with him. What do you say?" "I don't want you to leave me."

"Just remember that Papa and Big Momma will be with you every day, and they will take good care of you. You can even write me a letter every week. I will leave with you everything that you need to write me. You do print very well, remember?" "Yes Mama, Miss Rose said that I do some good writing." "Can I count on my little girl to say okay?" "Okay, Mama, you can go."

"Thank you baby for letting me go. When I get a job, and find a place for us to live, I will send for you and Papa." "Will it be a long time before I see you in New York?"

"I don't know how long it will be, but I will let you know every step of the way. Let's seal it with some love-kisses."

Mama reaches over and lifts me from my chair into her arms. She holds me so tight that I can hardly breathe as she kisses me more times than I can number. I don't feel sad any more. Mama says that everything is going to be all right. I believe her because she loves me and she tells the truth.

At one point, I felt that Mama didn't love me and that she was going to leave me alone with Papa and Big Momma without telling me.

CHAPTER VII

Living with Big Momma

The wind roared against our dining room window on this brisk November morning, as Mama and Papa gather my boxes of clothes to take across the road to Big Momma's house. They packed everything needed for who knows how long I will be staying over there. Mama says that she will send for Papa and me as soon as she is settled in New York. I really want to believe that she will come back for me and Papa soon.

It's nine o'clock in the morning. I am standing on the front porch watching Papa put both of Mama's suitcases (that she borrowed from Aunt Sadie Mae) in the trunk of his old car. Ropes are tied around them to keep them from popping open. Papa hollers at Mama as he slams the trunk close. "Eartha, are you ready? It's getting late." "I'll be right there when I finish packing my lunch box."

Mama walks out onto the porch all dressed up in her Sunday outfit. She looks so pretty. I still don't want her to leave me. She walks over to me and takes me by the hand, and walks me across the road. Big Momma had been watching all the action at my house from her rocking chair on the porch. She rises from her chair and walks over to the steps of the porch with outstretched arms to me. Mama releases her grip on my hand as she kneels down and wraps her arms around me. As she kisses me on my forehead, I see tears flowing from her eyes. I know that it's hard for her to leave us not because of fearing for our safety, but because she is going to miss us very much. Big Momma walks over to us and holds Mama in her arms for a long time. Neither of them says anything for a while. Then I hear her tell Mama, "Eartha, don't you worry about her, she is going to be just fine." Then she takes her by the hand and prays, "Dear Lord, please be with my daughter as she embarks on her new journey. We are thanking you in advance for taking her safely up north and giving her a job. Keep her in your care is my heart-felt prayer. God you said that we must ask, believing and You will answer our prayers."

We stand and watch as Mama goes back across the road to the car as Papa waits in the driver's seat. Mama keeps her eyes on me as long as she can. In a short time, Papa drives away from the house as we stand and watch them until they are out of sight. It will be a few hours before Papa gets back home.

Big Momma and I sit on the front porch for a while staring at the road toward the levy that Mama has to pass over to reach the train depot. After a short time of silence she sighs and says, "Oh well, life goes on." "Big Momma what do you mean?" "Child, no matter what we go through God is with us. He is going to take care of your Mama." "Big Momma, I am hungry, can I have something to eat?" "Of course, Lillimae, what would you like to eat?" "How about a biscuit, syrup and some fat back? I know that you always have some of that on hand after breakfast." "Sure, baby, you know what goes on in my house almost as well as I do. So you see, we're going to have a good time together."

She sets the plate on the table in front of me and before she sits down at the table with me, I began to eat. I take the biscuit and break off a small piece and sop up syrup and eat it. I love Big Momma's biscuits. In no time at all, I finish my brunch. Usually, I don't eat so fast, but because I'm a little nervous, I gulped down my food very fast. This is what happens when I don't know how to deal with situations that are very painful. After Brunch, me and Big Momma unpack my clothes boxes. She separates my clothes and places them in different dresser drawers: one drawer for socks, underwear, and slips; another one for my skirts and dresses. After we finish unpacking my clothes, we went back out on the porch and sat on the swing. Sitting on the swing is one of my most favorite times. Before long, I began to doze off and Big Momma, lovingly, takes my head and places it on her lap. I guess I must've slept for at least three hours. My sleeping gave her an opportunity to rest for a while too. Both of us begin to stir after a while. Big Momma is surprised that she rested for such a long period of time. I hear her speak quietly to herself that it is time to get up and start to prepare supper.

Grandpa will be home from work in a few hours, and she always has his meal prepared. It's one thing that I don't like about him, he drinks fire-water on Friday and Saturday night and Big Momma doesn't like that either. A long time ago when I slept over here, I heard them talking loudly about it. My Big Momma is a very quiet and soft spoken woman who loves the Lord with all her heart. She often says that God is keeping her through all of her struggles with him. Once I told Mama that Grandpa doesn't like Big Momma. She told me to shut my mouth, and that she never wants to hear me say such a thing again. So, from that time on, I never tell her anything about that. I don't like the way he talks to her when he doesn't think that I hear him. He thinks that I am asleep, but I hear everything that he says. Their bedroom is right next to the room where I sleep when I stay overnight. I love Grandpa, but he never tells me that he loves me. Sometimes he sits me on his lap and tells me stories about things that make me scared.

One night, as we were sitting on the porch swing, he told me that when the white man comes around every now and then to buy his scrap metal, they use it to make guns to kill black folk. I really didn't understand how he could sell something to somebody so that they could kill us with it. So the next time I saw the truck drive up to the house I would run and hide behind the house until it left. This went on for a long time. I kept this scary feeling to myself. I didn't even tell Big Momma about it. I wanted to tell Mama but I thought that I was forbidden to talk about them to anyone. So I kept it all to myself.

It's been two days since Mama left, and I don't know if my Papa will get home before I go to bed. Big Momma insists that I go to bed at seven o'clock because we have to get up early tomorrow morning and go to Sunday school at our church. Saturday night is bath night. Every day during the week I have a sponge bath. I can play in the bath tub on saturday nights as long as I want to. After Big Momma boils water on the wood stove in a great big iron pot, she takes it into the bathing room that is right off the kitchen, and pours it into the big tin tub that has some cold water already in it.

She makes the temperature just right for me by testing it with her elbow. This location, right next to the kitchen where it is warm, makes it easy for her to set-up the bath and the water stays warm longer. We don't have a room like this in my house. At home, I take my bath in the middle of my bedroom. Big Momma lets me bathe the same way Mama does. I wash myself and when I am finished, she comes in and washes my back, my private area, between my toes, and behind my ears. I don't know why I can't remember to wash behind my ears and between my toes. They always remember to wash these places for me.

After my bath, Mama usually braids my hair; she corn-rolled it on Friday night so that it will stay in place for at least all of next week. This way Big Momma won't have to do it for a while. Since my hair is so thick, and what Mama calls knotty, it usually takes her about two hours to wash and braid it. I am sure that Big Momma can do it just as good as Mama can: she taught her how to braid hair. After she helps me put on my night gown and my stocking cap, we both kneel down at the side of my bed and she prays that God would keep us all safe throughout the night, as He gives Mama traveling safety. One thing Big Momma and I know is that God is with my Mama during her travel. When she says, a-men, we both get up off our knees and she tucks me in and kisses me on my left cheek, and says "sweet dreams, child." Before long, I guess that I fell asleep because the next thing I hear is Big Momma in the kitchen preparing our Sunday morning breakfast.

What is going on in the kitchen reminds me of Papa's and my Sunday mornings with Mama. The same aroma of coffee brewing, frying bacon and oh those buttermilk biscuits that I love to sop up syrup with. I think that I am going to like living here for a little while. As soon as I wake up I run to the kitchen and ask for my Papa. Big Momma tells me that Papa will be over in a little while to have breakfast with us before we leave for Sunday school. She and grandpa had eaten breakfast already. He likes to get up early on Sunday mornings to catch up on the farm field and animal work that he doesn't get an opportunity to do during the week. He never goes to church with us. Big Momma is not happy about it, but she doesn't say anything about it anymore. She says that she is leaving him in the hands of the Lord.

I will refresh
the weary and
satisfy the faint.
–Jeremiah 31:25

own at the breakfast table, I hear the front screen
a's footsteps as he says in a loud voice, "morning,
to all." I jump up from the table and run to him.
h his strong arms and holds me tight to his chest
rl, I am so sorry that I couldn't be here to tuck
:now that Big Momma told you what happened."
ld me, I am just so glad to see you. Papa, Papa,
: that you won't ever leave me! You won't leave
)y girl, I promise you that I won't ever leave you.
going to make it my business to have dinner with
, and to tuck you in bed every night; how about
d for me, Papa." Papa says, "Now let us stop the
is great meal that Big Momma cooked for us so
:dy to go to church."

t my Mama with me seems very strange. I miss her
so much! I know that I won't have to miss her too long because she is
going to send money for Papa and me to go up north to live with her.
Sometimes I miss Mama so bad that I can't keep myself from crying.
Nobody will ever know that when I am alone I cry real hard into my
pillow. But when I am with people, I hide my tears because I am not
a baby. I am a big girl now and big girls don't cry in front of other
people. The face on my clock lets me know that it is seven o'clock
and I have to be ready for school at eight o'clock. Big Momma allows
me to wash my face and hands. When I finish, she comes into the
wash room and finishes my sponge bath. I clean my own teeth with
a corner of my wash rag that is dipped in a little baking soda that I
pour into my hand. It tastes nasty, but Mama says that it will keep
my teeth and gums healthy. I trust what my Mama tells me, because
she loves and cares for me. As soon as I finish cleaning my teeth Big
Momma says:

"Lillimae come now and eat your breakfast" "Big Momma I don't
like eating breakfast so early in the morning, it hurts my tummy."
"What are you talking about? You gotta have something in your
stomach so that you can be a good student." "I am already a good
student." "Child don't you get sassy with me, just eat your food." "I
am not hungry. Mama usually lets me eat a little bit and take the rest
with me to school for snack time." "Just eat a little bit and you can
take the rest to school. Is that okay?"

I don't want to upset Big Momma, but I just don't like eating so early in the morning.

When I am ready for school, my Aunt Sadie Mae stops by the house to pick me up to walk along with her and her girls to school. Both of them are older than me. I like getting to school early because my second grade teacher gives awards to the kids that are never late or absent. I have been present and on-time since school started in August. The last Friday of the month since school opened, four other girls and I with perfect attendance and punctuality received a reward from Ms. Cox. Not only do I get to school on-time, I get all A's in my classes too. Mama always tells me that I have to work really hard in school so that I won't have to pick cotton like she did. I remember the times that I was out there with her, and I saw her work so hard and sweat hard too. I never want to have to do that to pay the bills.

Most of the day my focus is on my school work, but on some occasions I find myself staring out of the window looking at the clouds in the sky and seeing Mama's face. It makes me sad, and I begin to wonder if she is all right. I know that she misses me as much as I miss her. I keep telling myself that I will see her soon. At the close of the school day the two o'clock bell rings and startles me back into reality. Each of us begins to chatter with each other as we gather our books and march in order out of the classroom.

Aunt Sadie Mae is waiting outside my school room door to pick me up and wait for her girls to meet at the big oak tree that sits in the middle of the school grounds. They arrive almost as soon as we get there. Each of them greet their mother with a kiss, my Mama is not here to greet me like that. Auntie loves me and she kisses me too, but it is not like my Mama's kiss. We share highlights of our day with each other as we walk over the hill to our houses. We arrive at our destination before we finish telling our stories of the day.

Big Momma is waiting for me at the door: She takes my books from me and kisses me on the forehead. "And how was my sweet grand baby's day?" "It was good."

"I have your snack on the table. Go and wash your hands, wash them real good now."

"Yes, Ma'am." I finish washing my hands as fast as I can so that I can eat. I am very hungry this time of the day. Usually Mama gives me a small snack because she wants me to eat a hearty supper.

When I reach the table I see that Big Momma made my favorite snack: two slices of light bread and a chunk of cheddar cheese, and a tin cup of milk. I eat so fast that Big Momma says, "slow down child, there is more where that came from."

Before I finish my snack she asks me if I have a lot of homework. "I don't have a lot of homework, just a little bit. Mama usually lets me do it by myself and then she checks it when I am done." "Is that how you want us to do it too?" "Yes ma'am, that is good."

I place my books on the kitchen table after I finish eating. All the kids in my class have a composition book for homework assignment. This way parents can see what we must do and they are asked to sign it when it is done. Ms. Cox knows that my Mama is not home with me to check my homework, and that Grandma or my Papa will sign my book.

The five o'clock whistle blows, and I know that in about an hour Grandpa will be home. He gets off work before my Papa does. I know this from the time that Mama taught me how to tell time. I hope that he don't fuss with Big Momma while I am living here. I know it won't be too long because Mama is going to send money for Papa and me to go up north. I am not a baby, I am a big girl now, and big girls don't cry. This is what I heard my friend's mother tell her when she dropped her off at school.

The cuckoo-clock chimes. I glance up to where it hangs on the front room wall and see that it is six o'clock. Grandpa will be walking over the levy in a few minutes. His boss-man drops his workers off at that spot every evening. I see him walking slowly toward the house. His long lanky legs get him to the house very fast. I holler to Big Momma that Grandpa is home, and I stand on the porch waiting for him to pick me up and tell me how happy he is to see me. He's not as loveable as my Papa is. He picks me up and gives me a tight hug and asks me, "How is my girl?"

"I am good Grandpa." He puts me down and walks into the kitchen to say howdy to Big Momma. He places his lunch box on the table and places a quick kiss on her cheek and goes straight to the wash room to wash up and change clothes for supper. After a little while, I hear Papa as he gives his quick three knocks on the door and walks right into the house. We never lock our doors, people are always welcome to our and Big Momma's house; not only that, there is always enough food prepared to feed anyone who comes by during meal-times.

Papa says, "How is my Precious baby girl today?" He puts his big strong hands under my arms and lifts me up to his face and gives me a kiss on my forehead. "I am good Papa. Big Momma checked my homework and she said that I did all of it good." "That's my smart baby girl, you keep on doing good and good things will come to you." "I will Papa; I promise that I will keep on doing good in school."

Papa goes into the wash room and prepares for dinner too. Mama made it clear to us that she wanted us to have our supper or dinner meals together. She understands how important this is for us to keep close to each other. Big Momma and Grandpa agree with her. This is how they raised all ten of their children until they got grown and moved out of the house.

After dinner, all four of us sit around the radio in the front room and listen to the Amos and Andy show. This is Grandpa's favorite radio program; Papa likes it too. As a family we sit together and listen to it without any talking: the segments are only fifteen minutes long. I am allowed to listen to it with them only if my homework is done. On church nights, Grandpa listens to the show all by himself because we go to Wednesday and Friday night meetings at our church.

My bedtime seems to come around too fast. Big Momma helps me with my bath as Papa and Grandpa spend some time together in the front room. I don't know what they talk about, but they do talk a lot. When I am ready for bed, I give Grandpa a good-night kiss and Papa takes me by the hand and leads me to my bedroom where we both kneel down next to my bed and pray that God protects us while we sleep. Also that He will keep Mama safe and give her a job so that we can be together soon as a whole family. I know that I am with family now, but it just ain't the same without Mama. Before Papa says a-men, it begins to thunder. I get scared when it thunders because last summer my best girlfriend was stricken by lighting after she tried to shield herself from the rain by taking shelter under a tree. Lighting split the tree right down the middle and electrocuted her. I was so sad about this and now I always think about her when there is thunder and lighting. I know, because Mama told me, that whenever there is thunder or lighting that I am supposed to find a quiet place, sit still, and pray for God to keep me safe.

Rain Drops On a Tin Roof

Tonight, of all nights, it is raining really hard. Fortunately, the roof didn't leak because Papa is a very good handy man and keeps the roof sealed. I like the sound of heavy rain drops falling on the tin roof of the house because the rain drops have a very soothing and comforting effect on me; it makes my sleep even more sweet and peaceful. The rain sounds like God's angels are ballet dancing on the roof. Only God can cause the sound they make with each step. Even though no one in Big Momma's house dances to worldly music, I believe that the Angels are dancing to God's miraculous music. I lay here, flat on my back in my bed thinking about how beautiful the sound of rain is to me. I am very comfortable knowing that God knows that I become afraid when I hear the thunder and see lighting flashing. He sends special Angels to dance over my head while they are watching over me and protecting me. After a while I am no longer aware of whether it is raining, lighting or thundering.

Once I fall asleep, I don't stir until I hear Big Momma encouraging me to wake up and get ready for school. There are no signs that we had a heavy rain fall last night. God is showing me that He understands what I feel even when it sounds crazy to my friends, and that I don't have to worry about anything because He is going to take care of me, my Mama and my Papa. I know that He is already taking care of Big Momma and Grandpa because she walks around the house saying, "Thank you Lord for taking care of me, my family and the family of God." So you see she is already protected and she knows that God is always taking care of her and the family.

Papa and I got two letters since Mama left for New York. It took two weeks for them to get here. We were so happy to hear from her. She told us that the train ride was more than four tiring days. She had many stopovers in some towns that I can't remember their names because the train broke down. It's been one month since Mama went up north and I am doing well in school and I sort of like living with Big Momma. She's a lot of fun to be with. She reads words from the Bible to me every night after supper. I can even recite some words by myself. This makes both of us smile: she smiles because of the Word, and I smile because I am going to get a piece of cake or peppermint candy from her. Since Big Momma rewards me for memorizing words from the Bible, I secretly learned the one hundredth Psalm all by myself. She was so proud of me that she showed me off to the Sunday school class. Not only did I get candy, but everybody told me how proud they were of me. The people in church made me feel real special too, just like my Mama did.

Roasted Sweet Potatoes

Roasting sweet potatoes in red hot fireplace ashes is one of my favorite things. Big Momma takes them from the sack and rubs them with grease that she saved after cooking fried fat back in a big black cast iron pot. When the meat is nice and crispy she takes it out of the pot and places each slice on a piece of brown paper to soak some of the oil out of them. After the grease in the pot cools off, she pours it into a tin can to use later on in cooking collard greens, cabbage, lima beans, black-eyed peas and snap peas. The flavor of meat left in the grease makes these foods taste real good. After greasing the potatoes, she places them in a small trough in the red hot ashes where they cook for about twenty minutes. Heat from the fire place makes the house warm and very cozy on these cold and damp evenings. Not only does the fire roast the potatoes, it really bakes the skin on my legs when I sit too close to it. After sitting so close to the fire for a few evenings, the skin on the front of my legs turns very dark and dry. After a week, it peels off almost like scales from a fish. Big Momma never told me that this was a problem; all she ever said was that I should not sit so close to the fire. I like sitting close to the fire because it makes me feel warm inside and outside too. Feeling cold makes me feel lonely and afraid that something bad is going to happen. These are the times that I want my Mama to hold me in her arms like she did before she went up north.

Soon this thought leaves me as Big Momma scoops ashes away from around the buried potatoes with a long-handled spoon (that Grandpa made for her) and places them in a tin flat pan after rinsing them off in boiling hot water. Then she dries them with a special towel, places them on a glass platter, splits them down the middle and places a dot of home-churned butter and a little sugar in them. This is my sweet treat for the evening before I go to bed. By the time she finishes preparing them, Papa and Grandpa come in after finishing their evening chores. They don't sit around the fire with us; instead they take at least two hot potatoes each and sit together and eat them at the kitchen table.

I sit on the floor at Big Momma's feet eating my hot sweet potato. It tastes so good, but I can only eat one. The last time I ate two of them I couldn't sleep because I had such a bad stomach ache. From that time, I eat only one at a time. Even early on I learned to listen to my tummy when it talked to me.

Big Momma in her rocking chair, and me sitting at her feet, we both enjoy our treat while she reads from her big black covered bible. She can eat and read between bites from it; even though she is always reminding me not to talk with food in my mouth. She reads stories about how God provides for the birds of the field and for us with His never-ending supply of what we need. Some of the words were too big for her to say because she never went to school; but she understood enough about the lessons from attending church that she would stop reading and just tell me the story. Teaching me God's Word is her responsibility and privilege. Many times, when I was in church, I heard our pastor say that parents ought to bring up their children knowing and living for Christ. After our snack and Bible reading time, Big Momma gives me a sponge bath and prepares me for bed. Papa, as he does every evening, prays with me and tucks me in before he goes across the road to our house for the night. In his prayers he always blesses Mama and prays that we will be together soon.

CHAPTER VIII

Mama's Train Ride to New York

Mama's Account of Her Painful Journey

Eighty three years after the end of the American Civil War, a train trip for black folks remains a humiliating, and sometimes harrowing experience. Lynching is still part of the Negro landscape, and we black folk know how to be careful about bringing extra attention to ourselves. My concern about Jim Crow segregation laws-named after a black character in minstrel shows–and travel restrictions, takes the excitement out of my new adventure. Many years ago Lucy Bell, my older sister shared stories with me about how badly black folks were treated in New York too. And how she traveled the same route that I did without any problems because she knew how to keep her mouth shut and play the game of survival. She knew what to expect, how to address white folks and how to stay in her place, and behave herself.

These words rang clear in my head as I settled down in the "Colored car" in my window seat for a life-changing trip: the ride of my new life from Dothan Alabama to Harlem New York.

I am fed up with having to sit in the back of the bus, ride in separate train compartments, and eat behind closed curtains in dining rooms. Sometime I think that it would have been better for me if I chose to move to Detroit instead of New York. At least there I can vote, sit side by side on streetcars, train, and buses without any restrictions because of my color. I can even drink water from the same drinking fountain and share rest rooms without discrimination. Most of my folk refer to Detroit as a "north-most southern city" or the "largest southern city in the United States." Since so many of us are moving there, the job market is very inviting and they hire us more easily too. Despite the absence of Jim–Crow laws there, we do suffer hate from the white man while he struggles to maintain white man rule, abuse us through police brutality and harassment, inadequate, and unavailable housing—that we cannot afford; bad school systems where they don't want us to learn our A,B,C's, and inferior jobs, just to keep us down. I am not prejudiced by any means. I am just aware of the reality of my station in life according to society. I know that God sees me in a totally different light. He sees me as a whole person made in His image and likeness. And because I care more about what He, my Heavenly Father thinks and knows about me, I don't fret because I know that God is my Defense-Protector. I refuse to hate my haters. A day for giving account of every thought and deed is coming for everyone who ever lived on God's good earth.

I have to stop thinking this way. God forgive me! I believe that You are preparing me to face a new way of living. When my sister made her first trip to the states she was scared, but it didn't stop her either. Anxiety and fear is not going to keep me from doing what I believe God wants me to do. Lord, speak to my heart by your Holy Spirit and your Word. I hear you telling me to move forward without doubt or fear. I know that you have not given me a spirit of fear but of love, peace and a sound mind. My mind is kept in perfect peace as long as I keep it stayed on you Lord. The enemy of my mind and heart is trying to hold me captive in a state of fear. I am sure to find my niche somewhere in that vast and beautiful place called New York.

Eartha in Harlem

The New York-bound train came to a quick stop at the New York Central Railroad Station. Being the only passenger in the Jim-Crow coach I sigh a loud sigh of relief; thinking of the times that I dreamed of this day. It is finally a reality instead of a dream. This, I know, is part of my God-ordained destiny.

Being the big woman that I am, it doesn't take much for me to grab hold of my suitcases and leave the train. I am so glad to be up north. The Red Cap can't even offer me a hand, but that's all right too. I can carry my suitcases and my almost empty shoebox that held my food for the trip. I ate everything that I packed for the Four Day trip except the cup of boiled salted peanuts. The smell of fried chicken surrounds me even though I ate it hours ago. My sister Lucy Bell knows the time of my arrival and I know that she will be there waiting for me. We have a practice in my family of showing up for appointments and specific occasion's hours before the time. As I look over the heads of so many white and black folks ahead of me I see my sister's head above all the rest. It's amazing that I can so easily recognize her in that we have not seen each other for more than ten years. One thing is for sure, everybody who knows Momma and Papa can recognize their children anywhere. If people outside the family can do that, surely we can do it more readily. Each of us has a strong resemblance to each other in height, complexion and body type. Both of my parents are over six feet tall. She and I are as tall as they are, and can be picked out easily in a crowd. We do make people take notice of us when we walk into a room. Not only because we are tall and what we call in the south "big boned" but we also talk loud and with a southern drawl. Our eyes catch each other and we rush pass other passengers to reach each other. Once we are within arms reach, I let go of my suitcase handles and rush into her arms. She hugs me so tight that it takes my breath away.

"Eartha, I am so glad to see that you got here safely. How was the trip?" Lucy Bell asks, hoping to hear that all went well, and that she didn't cause any trouble on the train.

"It was fine, I guess. I didn't get in any trouble with anyone, that's a good thing. It was the longest train ride in my life. It really was not a comfortable trip. I didn't like the idea of riding in a car all by myself."

"What do you mean, by yourself?" Lucy Bell asks.

"You know all about the segregation laws don't you?" Eartha smirks.

"Oh yeah!" I remember it well. "Segregation is more openly expressed down home."

"Enough talk about your trip. Are Big Momma and Papa getting along well?"

"They are well." She smiles, as thoughts of her baby girl—Lillimae crosses her mind, and she says, "God has been very good to us. You have to know that it took some convincing Ernest Lee to let me come up here."

"I bet it did. In that this is the first time that you all have ever been apart from each other." She replies.

"Come on and let us catch the Lexington Avenue train uptown to the house. We will hail a cab at 116th Street and Lexington Avenue to 119th and Madison: It's only about five blocks, but we can't walk it with your bags. And I can imagine just how tired you must be."

I am a little hesitant about riding a train that is under the ground. In Alabama it is called the Iron Horse you know. We rush down a flight of stairs as Lucy Bell hears the sound of an approaching train. I follow close behind her as she inserts a coin into the turn style, turns around after she enters and drops one in for me and I push my way through it. As soon as we get through the turn style our train pulls up in front of us. She tells me to step to the side of the doors as they automatically open and people rush off as if they are going to fight a fire. We stand aside to let people off, and then we rush in to find a seat just before the bells rings indicating that the doors are about to close. It's two o'clock on this November Sunday afternoon in 1948; (the last Sunday in the month) and there are many empty seats to choose from. Lucy Bells says that this is unlike that of the rush hour travel. This being my first time riding underground on the iron horse, I feel very uncomfortable about it. There's room enough for me to place my suitcases on an empty seat, but I stand them long side up on the floor to the right of my seat before I sit down. People are reading newspapers or paperback books; others are dozing with their heads bopping up and down or from side to side. I wonder how they do that without falling onto the floor. Here I am scared to death of the noise and screeching of the train wheels as the train turns and twists along the tracks through a dark tunnel, and these people are sleeping. This is my first time riding with so many people in one place at the same time. Wow, there are so many people–black, white and brown–riding peacefully on the train.

After what seems like an eternity, we arrive at 116th Street and Lexington Avenue Station. It takes a little time for my eyes to adjust to the light when we walk upstairs and out of the station. The sun seems exceptionally bright to me on this beautiful November afternoon. Taxicabs line the quiet street waiting to receive customers, and take them to their destinations.

Lucy Bell interrupts my train of thought as we wait for a cab to pull up in front of us when she says; "Sunday's ain't necessarily busy in this part of town. Most everybody gets up early and spends the whole day in church. We believe that Sunday is the Lord's Day, and we don't work or do anything except go to church." "You mean to tell me that you folks here, up north, set aside Sunday as a day of rest too?" Eartha asks with a hint of surprise in her voice.

"We sure do. Do you think that all of that good teaching that Big Momma taught us as children went to waste? I remember how we were taught in Sunday school, and at home, that we are not to work or do anything on Sunday that didn't please the Lord. It stuck with me to this day. I didn't go to Sunday school this morning because I wanted to meet you at the station. But I am going to evening service after I get you settled in. The church that I go to is directly across the street from my apartment building. It couldn't be any more convenient for me."

"You are right about that. You remember how far we used to have to walk through the woods, up and over the hill to get to church when we were kids?" "Yes I sure do!" she says. Before she says another word, a horn blast from a yellow cab that drives up to the curb to take us to what will be my home for an indefinite period of time.

"Come on Eartha let's get this taxicab before someone else takes it. In New York you have to push your way through or else you will be left behind. It's not like living down home where people are very courteous and look out for one another. But don't you worry about a thing; everything is going to be all right," she says as we rush across the sidewalk to the curb.

Lucy Bell smiles when she sees me struggling to the cab carrying my six feet height, and two hundred pound body frame. Fortunately, I have only two small old raggedy suit cases that hold my few clothes, and my shoebox that serves as my lunch box, with me. I know that when I find a job, I will buy a few more outfits from one of those well-known department stores on 34th street. One other thing that I know for sure, and that is, with the help of the Lord, I will never eat a meal from a shoebox again! "Are you okay?" "Yeah, I am fine." We enter the cab, and the driver says, "Where to folks?" "7281 Madison Avenue please, that's at the corner of 119th Street" Lucy Bell quickly replies.

CHAPTER IX

Life in Harlem

Early Sunday morning I awaken to the smell of fresh brewed coffee, smoked sausage, hominy grits, cheese eggs, and fresh baked biscuits. Lucy Bell didn't have to wake me up for breakfast; the aroma was the best alarm clock that I could have on this day. This morning, I am exceptionally hungry for a meal prepared by my oldest sister. Southern folk in the south always start the day off with a hearty hot breakfast. This kind of breakfast fuels our bodies sufficient enough to work the cotton fields on those twelve-hour days under the scorching Alabama sun. It's good to see that our family tradition still holds even here in my sister's home. Thinking about those days when I had to get up and out of the house before sunrise; and how it continued with a short midday break until dusk makes me shiver in anger for having to do it. But, with a sense of gratitude, I know that lifestyle is over for me forever! Having my daughter walking with me down those long rows, while I bend at the waist, and at other times kneeling, taking a firm grip on each of those fluffy puffs of cotton, and pulling them out of the thorny sheaths that caused my hands to look and feel like a man's hand, brings tears to my eyes. Thank God I will never, ever expose her or myself to that kind of lifestyle abuse again.

Before my thoughts go any deeper into my past field experience; I fall out of bed to the floor on my knees and give God thanks once again for being in a place that I have never been before; and for knowing that my cotton picking past will never be my present or future again. It is so freeing to know that I am on another journey to places that I can't even imagine. One thing I do know is that the Lord tells me in His Word that He will never leave me nor forsake me. I have enough faith to believe that these words are true. After communing with my God in Christ for about ten minutes I prepare myself for breakfast. Afterwards, my sister and I dress for, and leave for church.

Communion Sunday Service

This Sunday all the saints participate in Holy Communion Service at the United Church of Christ in Harlem. Bishop Onerous Nurse stands tall as he walks up and down the aisle proclaiming God's Word to the congregation. His oversized black doubled breasted suit jacket flaps back and forth exposing his white shirt that complements his wooly white, neatly trimmed hair. Mother Kelly Nurse makes sure that she picks up his heavily starched shirts from the Chinese laundry every Saturday morning so that he has at least five available for him to wear to each of the two or three services on Sunday. He also has one for each of the weekly services. Today, he seems to be sweating more than I've ever seen a man sweat in my whole life. None of this disturbs him because he sweats a lot even when he exerts himself singing, shouting and dancing in the spirit. All of a sudden, he shouts out to the 100-member congregation with a lisp, bathed in his thick southern accent, "Can we praise the Lord?" Almost immediately the congregation echoes back, "Hallelujah!" He repeats this question at least three times and the congregation responds likewise. Arms swinging in the air like an airplane, he walks up and down the aisle holding his well-used and tattered paperback Bible in his right hand and a dingy white towel to wipe perspiration from his face, hands and neck in his left.

Bishop Nurse's message captivates the congregation as he paints a picture of hope and deliverance from their pain and sorrow. He doesn't need a microphone because he says that God provides him with a built-in-one: his voice, every time he opens his mouth to glorify His name. Every so often, his voice gets so loud that I imagine it can be heard blocks away. At other times, it startles me to the point that I inconspicuously cover my ears with both hands to soften the blow:

I never want to bring attention to myself by doing this. Sitting at the rear of the church is helpful for me at these times, although I have heard people say that the back rows in church are for new comers, and backsliders. An usher, wearing her oversized white nurse's uniform, white laced shoes, cotton white stockings, and her head covered with a standard nurse's cap, sits at the church door to greet and seat parishioners.

Members of the congregation joyously acclaim "Amen" and "Hallelujah" as Bishop preaches a message of love and forgiveness. He says that, "I am setting you up for a blessing from God, while a clean heart is being created in each of you prior to receiving Holy Communion." Each member receives God's Word from him as he informs us that the bread and wine symbolizes the shed blood and broken body of our Lord Jesus Christ: this time he elaborates on this topic for all visitors, and reminds everyone of the seriousness of this part of the service. He left out the part that says that each of us must examine ourselves to see whether we are in the faith. Because if we take the bread and wine and our hearts are not right with God and man, we bring damnation upon ourselves. Lucy Bell whispers to me that he is too young for his memory to be failing him; he's only 64 years old. After three hours of worship and praise, it's finally time for benediction. Each parishioner instinctively closes their eyes and raises their hands toward heaven and repeat, after Bishop Nurse, "Lord Jesus keep us safe from all hurt, harm and danger; and may we take and apply the message we received today with us throughout the week." After this, the congregation sings "God be with you until we meet again." Everyone greets each other with a holy hug, handshake or a holy kiss, and goes their separate way. Most of them will return for the evening service that begins at seven o'clock.

CHAPTER X

Another Christmas Without Mama

It's been two years since I saw my Mama. She can't send for us yet because she has not made enough money to rent an apartment for herself and us. I know that it will happen soon. I am growing out of the new clothes that Mama bought me before she left for New York. Big Momma has a knack for making things work in her life just like my Mama does. She makes my clothes from flower sacks with beautiful floral patterns. Maybe the manufacturers know that my Papa and Big Momma can't buy me pretty dresses so they make pretty flour sacks for us to design and make our own dresses, slips, blouses and underwear. When she goes shopping for flour, she looks for sacks with a design that would look pretty on me. Pink and red are my favorite colors. Leftover pieces of the sacks (swatches) are set aside to be sewed into quilts for our beds. When my home-made quilt is not heavy enough to keep me warm at night, Big Momma takes clean clothes from the clothes bags and covers me up with them at night. These clothes, my portable bed covering, really keep me warm during these cold December nights. In the morning, I know that it is my responsibility to put these clothes in the clean laundry bag for future use. Every day before I leave for school, I clean up my room and leave it neat and in order. On the weekend, I have more time to play and take my time doing things that I have to do. I still have all of my dolls that must be put on the shelves that Grandpa made for me before I go to bed at night. I sleep with my doll that Mama gave me for my birthday before she went up north. I call her my *mama angel* because she watches over me every night with God and my Mama.

We are celebrating our third Christmas without Mama. Each year I help Big Momma make tree decorations. We take crepe paper and cut out garlands, trees and other figures to decorate the tree. Not only that, we make paper dolls, too. This is how we do it: I cut clean pages of paper on the straight line from my black composition book. Then I draw as many figures of a doll as I can on each page; after that, I take the scissors and pull on each arm and leg of the paper doll until it curls up. I draw faces on each of them and color the clothes on each of them. Strings are threaded through the head for hanging on the tree. These really make the tree pretty! Traditionally, without fail, on Christmas morning I get a bag with nuts, fruits and hard peppermint candy. Sometimes when I am chewing the peppermint candy it sounds like the candy speaks to me. It says, "Don't eat me." but I eat it any way. Candy is a rare treat for me because I have a home-cooked desert after every supper meal. There is no need, or hunger for eating in between meals since I eat four meals every day: breakfast, lunch, dinner and supper. I eat my last meal around 6 o'clock in the evening. All my meals are naturally farm grown, and large portions. No processed foods are eaten in our house except on rare occasions when Papa may bring home a loaf of light bread (bread sold in the store from a manufacturer). This bread is considered a treat in this house. Our daily drink with meals is either sweet tea, milk from our cows or water from the well. Only the older folk drink coffee. I hear that it may make me nervous and keep me from sleeping through the night.

I like school days for a lot of reasons. Since my family is so poor, a family member who works in the school cafeteria makes sure that I get a free lunch pass every day. Big Momma's food is good, but it seems like the food at school tastes even better; especially when I am eating with Baby Doll, my best friend. Lunch at school is like supper at home. Being poor does not mean that I am not eating balanced meals. Even poor folk in my town eat good food. Big Momma must have taught Mama how to plan and cook good meals: I guess that God taught Big Momma how to cook. She tells me that God will show me how to do all things well. Somebody in my church who lived in the north says that children who don't eat good food have trouble making babies, and keeping them inside until they grow enough to live outside the body. Well, I see a lot of mommies with big tummies and a lot of babies too. I think that all of us eat good food in my school and my church. I like babies, and when I get married, I want to have a lot of them.

CHAPTER XI

Life Without My Family

Alone without my husband and child, I am feeling a little down this evening, and I don't think that I will be going back to church this evening. My thoughts are on Ernest Lee and my baby girl. I miss them so much. Suddenly I feel the need to pray for both of them and my Momma and Papa. I see them in my mind's eye getting themselves ready for evening service at my church in Alabama. We looked forward to these special times together with other believers. Tonight, I don't really feel uplifted in my spirit even though I had a wonderful time in the Lord all day up to this time. It has finally hit me that I don't have a job yet and my family won't be able to come up north until I can afford my own place and enough money to send for them.

After service today, I just feel like being alone in my room praying and seeking God's direction about finding a job. Questions keep coming to my mind such as; what kind of job can I do here, who is going to hire me without any experience, will I make enough money to take care of myself and my family until Ernest Lee gets a job? Before my doubts and fears got the best of me Lucy Bell knocks on the frame of the door to my room. You see, living in a flat, there are no doors to separate one room from the other. Curtains hang from the top of the door frame to provide a sense of privacy. When the curtains are closed, it means that the occupant is trying to have some private time desiring not to be disturbed. On occasion, roomers have to exit the flat through the front door and walk through the long hallway to enter the kitchen at the end (back) to use the rest room or get something from the kitchen. Everyone in the flat must walk through each room to get to the kitchen, front room and the rest room. In essence each person living in the flat (apartment) respects the other's need for privacy as best as they can.

Lucy Bell says, "Eartha, are you going back to evening service?" "I don't think that I will tonight." "Are you feeling well? You seem to be a little preoccupied this evening. Is there something that I can help you with?" "You know that it's been two years since I've been here and I still don't have a job." "I know that Eartha, just be patient, something will come through for you." "I know that it will, but when? I miss my family so much, you must know that! I am so grateful for everything that you are doing for me." "Don't worry; it won't be long before you get the job that will unite you and your family. Why don't you stay home tonight and write letters to them letting them know that you are all right." "That sounds like a good idea. Lillimae would love to have her own personal letter from me. She reads quite well you know."

It's eight o'clock and I am home alone and feeling a bit tired. I really don't feel up to writing letters tonight, but I guess that there will be no better time to do it. So, with pencil and writing pad in hand I start writing. First I write a note to my baby girl telling her how much I miss her, and that we will be together soon. To my most favorite man in the whole world I write a sensual love letter expressing what he knows that we have in common. However, I am getting to be a little concern about his sexual fidelity to me. I know that I miss our intimate times together and find it very difficult to handle. This is one of the reasons why I spend so much time in church and in prayer. I am really trying to keep my body under subjection to the power and will of God as a Christian wife who has been physically separated from my husband. My letter to Momma and Papa informs them that all is well and my prayer request is they pray that I get a job soon. When I finish writing my letters, I feel so relieved that I get myself together and go across the street to evening service. The clock on the front room wall chimes indicating that it is nine o'clock. Church services on Sunday evenings usually dismiss around eleven o'clock. I don't like getting to church late. However, tonight I am not bothered by that at all. God has given me a sense of peace in my heart, and a witness in my spirit that I am going to get a job this week.

Finding a job

A sense of expectancy is so alive in me that I can shout it from the house top. I know that testimony service is over by now, but I give God thanks before I enter the church for what He has already done for me. Oh my, I hear words of faith and assurance rising up in me that says the effectual fervent prayers of the righteous man/woman avails much. I know that in and of myself, there is no righteousness. However, I have the righteousness of God working through His son Jesus in my life. What liberty, what freedom, what joy in knowing that God is working all things out for my good and His eternal purpose. I know, without a shadow of a doubt, that I was lead by the Spirit of God to leave my job and family in Alabama and move here. No, no, I will not allow the devil to cause me to think otherwise. The light from the Lord that I received must continue to shine in and through me when I feel like I am in a dark place. Before writing those letters, I felt like I was trapped in a dark bubble of despair. Faith and obedience in what I may consider insignificant is the key that opens the flow of blessings from the vessels of Heaven's store. When God opens the windows of Heaven and pours out His blessings there may not be room enough to receive all of them. These words really refresh my spirit and incite me to sing words from a song: I feel like going on, I feel like going on, though trials come on every hand, I feel like going on. Thank you Jesus!

Would you believe it? That very day after I received the witness and peace in my spirit God openly rewarded me with an answer to my prayer: a letter from a job I interviewed for three weeks ago offering me a job. It was mailed to me one day last week, and I received it today. God had already prepared a particular employer downtown to hire me–a particular woman, to work on a particular job in a particular factory. My interview for this particular job went very well: but since I hadn't heard from the owner sooner, I assumed that I didn't get the job. God's timing is perfect! I will start my new factory job next Wednesday at six o'clock in the morning. I am so happy! Now I can make things ready for my family to come up north so that we can be together again the way God meant us to be.

Six Months Later (May 1951)

My job is working out well. However, I haven't saved enough money yet to find an apartment and send for my family. The situation is beginning to make me doubt whether I made the right decision to leave my family and come up here. Lucy Bell is so sweet and encouraging to me. She said that she would loan me the money that I needed, but I don't like to borrow money from anyone. I remember Momma's words, "Never borrow money unless you know without a shadow of a doubt that you will be able to pay it back as soon as possible." I don't want us to start out owing money to my loving and caring sister, and not being able to pay her back. She deserves better than that. I will just keep on saving until there is enough money for me to do what I need to do. My few dollars are adding up, and it won't be long before I will be able to be with my family again.

I overheard one of our neighbors say that there was a woman, just like me, who came to New York to establish a new way of living for herself and her family who couldn't make enough money on her own. She got involved with a married man who owned his own business and had lots of money. This woman, because of her love for money and lack of patience to wait on the Lord, lost her self-respect, the respect of others and most of all her family. Like the Bible says, the love of money is the root of all evil. There is no way, with the help of the Lord, that I could put myself into such a compromising position! Nothing or nobody is more important to me than my relationship with my Lord and my family. I am going to wait on the Lord and be encouraged while I am waiting. Sometimes my faith wavers a little, but I am going to hold on to my faith. It has worked for me and I know that Jesus never fails. The failure is in me when I doubt the Lord. I ask God to increase my faith; I know that I have to do my part also: pray, fast, read and obey God's Word.

CHAPTER XII

Tickets To Ride

After "saving every dime that she could save", that's what Mama writes in her letters to me, she finally saves enough money to send for Papa and me to come up north. The mailman delivers a registered letter to Big Momma with two one-way train tickets to New York, and a hundred dollar money order for us. It excites me so much that I will be riding on the iron horse to New York to be with my Mama that I start crying, and my appetite for supper goes away. I can't believe that I am crying and not in pain or getting a whipping for something I did that was not right. I remember when Mama was here, she talked about tears of joy; I didn't know what she meant then, now I understand what it means. It feels so good! I can't wait until Papa gets home from work to let him know that we will be leaving soon to be with Mama. All that I am feeling makes my heart beat fast and my breathing too; but it doesn't hurt. When Papa gets home he reads to me what the tickets say; Big Momma can't read all the big words.

"Baby girl, August 31st is our big day."

"For real Papa, we are really going up north?"

"Yes, it's all real; we will be leaving on the thirty-first on a four day train ride. We will ride on the same train that Eartha Mae did: the Silver Star to the New York Central Railroad."

"What day are we leaving?"

"Well, today is Thursday August 17th; we have two weeks to get everything in order."

"I can't wait; I will start getting my stuff together now."

"Hold on there, baby girl, we will just take the things that we have to, and have the rest sent to us. I have to get us a few suitcases and a few boxes to pack our belongings in."

"Papa, Papa, I love you so much, and I am so happy today. I think this is the best day ever in my life."

All of a sudden I realize that Big Momma is not in the room with us. I guess while I was busy talking with Papa she went to her room and sat in her rocking chair that sits next to the window. Immediately, a little sad feeling came in my heart. For a little bit of time I forgot about her. I love Big Momma too. She takes good care of us just like Mama did before she went away. Is Big Momma going to miss us the same way I missed Mama? Oh, how much she is going to hurt. I was hurt real bad for a long time after Mama left us. When I go into Big Momma's room I see her sitting in her favorite prayer and Word reading chair rocking herself back and forth without saying a word. I kneel at her feet and look into her golden-brown eyes that are so bright and pretty. Some people say that her eyes are too light for her bronze skin color. She is so soft and pretty to me.

"Big Momma, I love you, and I am going to miss you. One day I will come back to see you, I promise. I promise."

"Sure you will baby, and you know how much I m going to miss you. You are like my very own child. Just remember you had a good upbringing here, and I pray that you will always remember that you are a very special child, and that greatness is ahead of you as long as you walk right."

"Yes, ma'am, I am going to make you proud of me."

"Baby, I am already proud of you."

"I know, but I am going to make you even more proud, you just wait and see!"

Big Momma beckons me to get up from the floor and sit on her lap. Although, I am a big girl she still holds me on her lap the same way she did when I was a little girl. I think that she gave me extra servings of love because my Mama wasn't here to give it to me. Grandpa is very stiff with me, but Big Momma likes to hold me in her arms, hug me close to her heart, and kiss me on my forehead. I really like being held close to her chest. I suppose that it reminds me of those months that I spent inside Mama's womb, my shelter from the storms.

"Do you know that in two weeks me and Papa are going away?"

"Yea, I know, and I will miss you both so much. God will take you to your new home without any hurt, harm or danger. He will be with you through every storm of life that He allows you to ride. Just ride it knowing that you are never alone. Can you promise me that you will remember to lean on Him, just as you are leaning on my chest right now?"

"Yes ma'am, I will remember."

This is the morning, the Thursday morning that I have been waiting three years for. The past two weeks have been the longest weeks in my life. It seemed like today would never arrive. Well, it is here and I am going to be with my Mama. It's really true, and I am not dreaming like I did for the last three years of this day. Grandpa is driving us to the train depot for our trip of a lifetime. Big Momma sits quietly next to me in the back seat of the car. I bet that she is quietly praying about many things because that is just what she does. All my doubts and fears are gone. It's really happening, oh, boy, it's really happening to me! In four days I will be with my Mama.

CHAPTER XIII

Never Enough Money

One Year Later (November 1952)

Mama's Self-Talk

A whole year has passed by and I am singing the same tune: "Not enough money! I never have enough money to take care of my responsibilities. It has been six months since my family's arrival. What a happy day it was when I saw their beautiful faces. My little girl had grown-up to be quite a young lady. Ernest Lee had put on quite a few pounds, yet he remains as handsome as ever. Early on, we were so involved with each other that one would think that we were on a second honeymoon. After a couple of weeks together and he being without a job and too much free time on his hands he became somewhat distant from me. Maybe it is my imagination because I am so tired and disturbed that he has not found a job. And, I believe that he could be more diligent in looking for one. He is not the happy man that I lived with in Alabama. Again, I question whether I made the right decision in moving up north! I am sure that, in time, I will have no doubt about the move. Unfortunately, Ernest Lee hasn't found a job since he and our daughter arrived here six months ago. Not only am I responsible for paying the rent on our two-bedroom apartment; buying food and clothing, but also my monthly subway ticket. Now, my mind seems to be playing tricks with me. The first thing I do when I get paid on Friday is to set aside my tithes and offerings for the week and purchase my subway ticket. I know my priorities! Thank God that we are just one block away from Lucy Bell, and she is such a big help to us in terms of baby sitting and preparing meals for us. Sunday dinners are always at her house; and she refuses to take any help from us. She's a sensitive and very giving woman. I believe that is why God blesses her so much: she gives unselfishly to others of her substances in an attempt to alleviate the suffering of others without expecting anything in return. People can show up at her flat any time of the day or night and she will feed them if they are hungry and make room for them if they need a place to sleep. Her cupboard is never empty.

Complaining about my financial situation is not what I want to do. I must ask myself, is it all about my finances or something more disturbing than that? Sometimes I just can't help myself. I am hesitant to share my innermost thoughts about our finances or our relationship changes with Ernest Lee because I am afraid he will say that it was not his idea in the first place that we make this move. He was satisfied with the way life was going for us when we lived down south. I am sure that we are going to be all right here; we just have to be patient with ourselves and each other, and trust God's hand in our present situation. "I have got to get out of this financial hole that I'm in."

Lillimae's Observation

I overhear Mama talking to herself as she peeks through the window blinds waiting for the Saturday mail truck to arrive. As soon as she sees it, she throws her winter coat over her shoulders and dashes out to meet it in her flannel night gown and slippers, yet wearing her stocking cap on her head to keep her hair in place. Before the mail carrier can put the mail in the mail box, she dashes up to the truck and grabs the mail from his hand hoping to see a letter from her employer offering Papa a job at the factory where she works. Anxiously, she looks through the mail for an envelope with his name and her job's letterhead. She says, "It's not here, maybe it will come on Monday." She rushes back into our ground floor apartment with a sad face.

Here, I am sitting at the table that has unopened mail and newspapers from the past week that Mama doesn't have time enough to read. Papa is not available much of the time. Mama says that he is out looking for any job that will help pay the bills. I miss him a lot. Things are not like they were when we were down south. There, after supper, we spent some time together before he tucked me into bed. Sometimes Mama seems to be mad with me and Papa: Like today, before I finished eating my brunch (peanut butter and jelly sandwich) she raises her voice saying, "Child hurry up and finish your brunch so that I can figure out how I am going to pay this month's bills. These bills are driving me mad. What am I going to do?" I watch her struggling trying to figure out how she is going to pay all her bills. I dare not get sassy with her because she keeps a switch (thin tree limb) in view that speaks for itself. Remembering how it can sting my bare legs helps me to keep my mouth shut. Mama believes that to spare the rod is to spoil the child. I am not a spoiled nine year-old because the rod (switch) has not been spared but used when necessary. Papa doesn't seem to understand how sad it makes Mama feel when she can't pay all of the bills by herself.

Paying the Bills

Mama is sitting at the kitchen table wearing her overly washed, faded pink flannel night gown and her stocking cap. An exposed, 40-watt light bulb directly overhead provides her with hardly enough light to read her statements and fill out the money orders correctly. She doesn't like to open the blinds this early in the morning; our apartment is on the street level, and she values our privacy. She thinks "Here goes three hours of stress trying to rob Peter to pay Paul on my meager salary." The smell of fresh brewed caffeinated coffee permeates the air of our small apartment as she sits sipping the steaming hot beverage from a chipped ceramic cup inscribed with her and my names written in bright red print. She repeats one of her most frequently used words, "Not enough money! Yesterday was payday and here today it has already been spent: I never have enough money to take care of my responsibilities; I've got to do something to get myself out of this financial hole." Dear Lord, please let my boss give Ernest Lee a job. I know that you know all about our struggles. Please forgive me for what others may see as an attitude of ingratitude. I thank you for all that you have done and what you are doing even as I breathe this word of prayer. For I know without a shadow of a doubt that my prayers are heard and that you answer according to your time and good pleasure. Help me Lord to know how to wait and be encouraged and joyful while I am waiting. You said in the Word that I am not to be anxious about anything, but to pray about everything. I confess that I am feeling fearful about my situation, and I know that these feelings can open me up to Satan's attack. I pray this prayer in faith, believing that my family's blessing has already been dispatched. You did it before for me, please do it again.

Two Men in White Coats

Picture this experience through the eyes of a 9 year old child. The sound of my Mama awakens me in the middle of the night. She is screaming at the top of her lungs uncontrollably while, she jumps up and down on the bed as if she's on a trampoline: her head almost hitting the high dirty white ceiling. Papa is trying to calm her so that she doesn't hurt herself or wake the residents of the entire building which houses four other families. Unfortunately, he is unable to calm or control her screams or her erratic bodily movements. All of a sudden I hear sirens from police cars, and an ambulance approaching the building with flashing red lights that light up the entire block. Now the whole community will know that something is wrong with my family.

When I was a little girl growing up in Alabama, my Mama and my Big Momma stressed the importance of keeping family matters (secrets) within the family. I suppose that is why having strong family ties are so important to me even as a nine year old little girl.

Papa tries his best to keep me away from the drama that is taking place right in front of my eyes and ears. I hear and see it all! I think that I will remember this night for the rest of my life. This picture will live vividly in my mind forever! Out of nowhere, it seems, two men in "white coats" catch Mama during one of her leaps toward the ceiling, wraps her in a white sheet that has sleeves on it, and takes her away. Papa and I are left wondering what is going on here? Where are those "white men" in "white coats" taking my Mama after wrapping her in the "white sheet with sleeves?" She doesn't look like my Mama; she looks like a scared little girl as her tear-filled eyes catches mine. I am left standing at the door with Papa, I am crying and shouting, "Don't take my Mama away, please, don't take my Mama away."

Mama stays in the hospital for a long time. Papa tells me that she needs some time to rest. I hear Aunt Lucy Bell telling the people in the church to pray for her healing of a nervous breakdown. It doesn't matter to me what they call it, I just want her to come home. I miss her so much! When she comes home from the hospital no one talks to me about what happened to her. I didn't see her during all the time that she was away. Papa and Auntie Lucy Bell always told me that Mama sends her love and kisses to me; and messages telling me that she will be home soon. Her soon to me was a very, very long time, although I like staying with auntie.

While Mama was in the hospital, Papa was hired by her boss who was very sorry about her being sick. He assured him that her job was safe in that she is a valued employee. Now both of them will be working in the same place. This news increased her faith and joy in knowing that God answered her prayer, and that she was no longer solely responsible for meeting the financial needs of the family. It is good for me to know that my Mama and my Papa will be able to sit down together at our kitchen table, and figure out how to pay the bills.

Chapter XIV

Lifes' Perspective From Lillimae

(Age 14 yrs)

Mama and Papa continue to work very well together on their job. He works the evening shift and Mama continues to work from six in the morning until two o'clock in the afternoon. These hours are good for her in that she is home early enough to receive us from school, help us with our homework, feed us dinner, and prepare us for bed. When I was just a little girl I didn't want to share my parents with sisters or brothers. Now I am a teenager with three siblings: two sisters and one brother (Mama had a baby every year since Papa and I arrived). Mama and Papa like the idea of having a big family, especially since Mama only missed two weeks of work with each pregnancy; and that was after her deliveries. Thank God Aunt Lucy Bell was available to help her with us especially when the babies were small.

Now I have the responsibility of making sure that everyone gets off to school on time or to Aunt Lucy Bell's flat around the corner. It wasn't smart of me to think that I would be an only child because Mama has nine siblings; and children from happy families often like to continue that pattern for living. Now I am having second thoughts about having a lot of children when I get married. It takes a lot of time, money and patience to raise well-rounded, Godly children. Only time will tell how my life is going to turn out.

My siblings and I are seeing less and less of Papa these last few weeks.

When Papa lived down south he was well respected on his job. Everyone knew that he was a Minister of the Gospel and highly respected by his boss and everyone who knew him and our family. We were considered important to our people. If he needed extra time off for church funerals, weddings or any other reason his requests were never denied. Papa worked his job as unto the Lord because he believed that great rewards would be granted from the Lord. The boss even allowed him to lead a short prayer time with the men before they started work. My Papa really felt good about himself when he was allowed to do what he had a heart to do. I feel like he's sad because people here don't like him, and he can't do or say the things for God the way he used to. Some people even laugh at him because of the way he talks. I heard him tell Mama about that when he first started working on her job. We still go to church here, but it is not the same. I miss the good times we had back home. Things are so different now. I don't like it!

Papa is supposed to get home every morning from his night job to get us off to school and to aunties apartment. Yesterday he got home two hours later than usual. I smelled alcohol on his breath, and his eyes were very red. He walked past me without saying a word and went straight to bed. I know all about what alcohol can do to people because I saw what it did to a few people in my family when I lived down south. Apparently, on Friday nights and all day Saturday, many people in my immediate family drank liquor to relax and forget about the hard time they had during their work week.

One Saturday, in the middle of the day, I walked into a family member's home and saw her and her boyfriend sleeping on their bed after a Friday night of drinking alcohol, and smoking cigarettes. Unfortunately for me, I saw his private part and quickly left the room without awakening them. I never saw anything like that before, but I guess that I knew that it was something that I should not have seen. Maybe I related it to statements such as, "keep your dress down and your panties up," don't let anyone touch you down there" that I heard spoken by Mama, Big Momma, and older girl cousins and my auntie over the years. They were not addressing these words specifically to me, but to older girls in the family and the church. I knew that private parts were to be kept hidden from public view. Only my parents and Big Momma could see my private when they helped me with my bath. As a little five-year old girl, I knew that I shouldn't be seeing such a thing. This was the first time I saw an adult's private part; I had seen babies during their diaper change and I thought nothing of it. But this was a little frightening. From that day to this one, I never enter a room without knocking or announcing myself first. Even though Big Momma always talked about the sin of drinking alcohol and smoking cigarettes, at least four of her children didn't listen to her and did it anyway. She was so happy that her daughter Eartha, my Mama, married a minister: this way she would not have to suffer the same ugliness in marriage that she did.

I wonder what made my Papa drink last night. Is it possible that he has been drinking all along and I didn't know it, or did he just start here in New York? He is supposed to be a man of God who preached against drinking alcohol, smoking cigarettes and dipping snuff. Could it be that my Papa is a hypocrite? It is very hard for me to even think this way. How is this going to affect my Mama? She had a break-down a few years ago. God knows that I don't want her to go through what she went through again. I am not going to tell her that Papa is not coming home as early in the morning as usual, and that the smell of alcohol and cigarettes are all over him. This happens on Tuesday and Thursday mornings. He gets paid on Thursday mornings before leaving work. The smell of alcohol makes me feel like I am going to throw-up; and brings back memories of that Saturday morning in my aunt's house when I was just a little five-year old child. I felt so ashamed and scared to tell Mama about it. It is hard for me to carry these secrets about him and not say anything to my hardworking Mama. My siblings are too young to understand what is going on so I don't worry that they will tell her. I don't like him the way I used too; he does not care very much for us either. Why is he doing this to us? I am feeling very sad and tired. Who can I talk to about what is going on in my family? Should I write a letter to Big Momma? What if she tells Mama and she gets upset with me. My Mama is my best person in the whole world and I don't want to do or say anything to hurt her and our closeness. These words are ringing in my ear, "Pray, pray, you know that prayer works." For nine long months, back in 1942 I was bathed in prayer while hidden in my Mama's womb. If it worked then, I know that it will work for me today. Who would have thought that I would ever have the need to pray this kind of prayer?

God's Word says that the heart is desperately wicked, who can know it. Only God knows what's in the heart of man. He knew way back then what my Mama and Papa would be doing today. I knew that they should not have more children: I wanted to be their only child. Maybe, they would be happy, like before, if they only had to dress, feed and take care of me until I become grown and able to take care of myself.

Keeping my secret about Papa's staying out most of the early morning is beginning to upset my stomach. Every day before I go to school my stomach feels like someone is stabbing a very sharp knife into it. When I get these pains it feels like I need to use the toilet, but I don't. What am I going to do? As soon as the school bell rings at three o'clock I feel the same stabbing pain. Thank goodness that I live only a five minute walk from the school.

Park Avenue is shinning bright as I leave school through a side door. At three o'clock in the afternoon, the sun is warm even though it is the first week of February. I run home as fast as my long legs can carry me holding my book bag tight in my hand. As soon as I reach my first floor apartment door I push it open with as much strength as I can muster after running all the way home. We never lock our doors, which is a good thing for me today since I am in a hurry. When I arrive home I run past Mama to the toilet; not only do I feel the pain in my stomach, it feels like a train is running through my gut too.

"What's the matter, child?" Mama says as she moves aside to let me pass. Usually, we greet each other at the door with a hug and a kiss. My sisters and my brother are oblivious to my presence as far as I can tell. My thoughts are not on them at this time either! Papa is usually sleeping when Mama gets home from work and he remains asleep until dinner time. All of us usually sit down together at the kitchen table and eat our meals together as a family. Table-talk-time gives each of us an opportunity to talk about any thing that we want to that happened during the day. Each of us receives both positive and negative feed-back from them. We know what to do, how to do it, and what will happen to us if we don't follow instructions specifically as they are given to us. These times are really important to me: they bring back memories of our good times when we were living down south.

Mama follows me to the toilet. "Baby, are you okay?" she says as she opens the door. We don't lock doors in our apartment. She reaches over and touches my forehead to feel for signs of a fever. She says, "You don't feel hot. Do you think that you ate something in school that upset your stomach?"

"No Mama, my stomach was hurting before I left for school today. It has been hurting me for a long time, but it is worse today than before." "Are your bowels moving right?"

"Yes Mama, they're working well." She leaves me and heads back to the kitchen to finish preparing dinner. "I am feeling a little better now, Mama." "I will make you a cup of mint tea; maybe it will make you feel much better." "I like the way you and Big Momma make mint tea with a lot of sugar; it always makes my stomach feel better." Before I leave the toilet, the thought of Papa crosses my mind, and the pain gets stronger. Every time I think about what he did my stomach begins to hurt. I pick up my school bag and head to the bedroom that I share with my sisters and brother. All of a sudden I notice that Mama and Papa's bedroom door is open. Usually, when we come home he is asleep in the room with the door closed. That's why we are taught not to make too much noise so that he can get his rest before dinner. After dinner, we usually spend some time together before he and Mama relax together in bed before he leaves for work at ten o'clock.

Mama calls me to the kitchen to have my cup of tea. "Now, baby, sit down and drink your tea while it is hot. It will make you feel better, and if your pain doesn't go away I may have to take you to the doctor. Something is going on in your cute little body, and we are going to find out what it is!"

My self-talk says, "If she only knew what is causing my pain it would cause her pain too." Once I heard the preacher say, "We are as sick as the secrets we keep." Maybe this is why the pain in my stomach hurts so bad. I have got to tell somebody about what Papa is doing! To relieve my curiosity, I ask Mama, "Where is Papa, it's after six o'clock and he's not home yet?" "Baby, your Papa left me a note telling me that he is putting in some overtime today, and that he will be home before you all go to bed." "That's good Mama, I miss Papa so much." "I can tell that you are feeling better."

"Yes, Mama, I feel much better, the tea helps a lot." "Why don't you do your homework now, dinner will be ready in about half an hour." In less than thirty minutes I finished my homework because I did most of it in school during my lunch time. Mama keeps my sisters and brother busy in our room during homework time.

After dinner Mama and I clean up the kitchen and prepare the bath tub in the kitchen for our baths. The bath tub's cover doubles as a counter top in the kitchen. Papa usually removes the cover for us because it weighs about ten pounds. It's pretty heavy for us to remove, but we do it together without a problem. My sisters and I bathe together first, then I wash the bath tub and prepare it for my brother. Thank God we can stay up until 10 o'clock on Friday nights and sleep late on Saturday mornings unless something special is happening at the church. Sleeping late and eating a Mama-cooked breakfast is better than eating Papa's thick, tasteless oatmeal or his lumpy hominy grits during the week. Tomorrow we can sleep late and have Mama's big week-end breakfast of whatever we want. I prefer flap jacks with molasses mixed with a little bit of grease from crispy fried fat back, and fried eggs. My sisters and baby brother like Kayro syrup on their flap jacks, they hate the taste of molasses. Mama and Papa will eat whatever she cooks for us and our leftovers with their coffee. We children are not allowed to drink coffee: it makes us nervous.

As soon as I think about sleeping late and having a good Mama-cooked breakfast in the morning, Papa enters the apartment smelling like alcohol again. His eyes are blood shot, and he is unsteady on his feet. I have never seen him like this before. Mama looks at him as if a monster or ghost appeared before her eyes. Before saying a word to him, she rushes us off to our bedroom as if to protect us from something bad. I think that I know what is going on with my Papa because of how he has been acting over the past few weeks. Maybe I won't have to hold my secrets about him from Mama any longer. He is telling her himself what he has been doing when she is at work.

"Got to wash up," he says, and goes straight to the toilet. He locks the door and the next thing we all hear is him retching and vomiting so forcefully that it startles us. We run out the room to see what is happening but Mama motions for us to go back into our room. Lying still on our beds, we listen for Papa to be all right. It is very difficult for us to go to sleep because we are scared for Papa. We just lay quietly in bed not knowing what is going to happen next, all of this is very new to us. My Papa is a believer. He and Mama have been working together in ministry since they were married fifteen years ago. Now, I fear that something bad is going to happen to us. Papa is not the same since he started working at Mama's job. I thought that when he got a job and started to make money that he and Mama would be happy. He is far from being happy! I remember hearing his say a long time ago that his Papa left his mother alone to care for his sisters and brothers when he was a little boy. Oh God, please don't let him do the same thing to us.

I have to keep the kids quiet while Mama is helping Papa get himself together. Thank God that before long they fall asleep. When they do, I put my ear to the wall trying to hear what is going on in their bedroom. "Let me help you undress for bed," she says to him. "I don't want to go to bed now. I love you, don't you know I do?" "Yes, yes, I know." "Listen, just let me help you, we don't want to disturb the children." "Fine, fine, go ahead and help me!" "I'll leave your underwear on, and you go to sleep. We will talk tomorrow when you are sober. "What do you mean sober?" "We will talk about it tomorrow. You just go to sleep now."

In a few minute I hear Papa snoring louder than any noise I ever heard coming from a human being. It is surprising that the kids can sleep through all of this noise. Now that he is asleep, I want to go to her and love on her: but I am afraid that I might tell her the secrets that have been making me sick for weeks. I'll just try to go to sleep now; God will give Mama everything she needs to deal with Papa's problem.

CHAPTER XV

Mama's State Of Confusion

Again, I ask myself, was I out of order when I made a decision to leave the south and move here? I am feeling confused, frightened and betrayed by the man that I love; the man that I thought would be by my side through thick and thin. Well, I see now that we are in the thick of things and I really don't know how we got here. This can't be the first time he has done such a crazy thing. My husband, the believer, drunk! I can't believe it! I wonder how many times he let himself go to drink alcohol to the point of getting drunk: and what else is he doing that I am not aware of while I am out working trying to help him take care of our family? What is bothering him to the point that he gave himself over to the influence of the enemy? Did he not know that there are consequences to his behavior; especially since he is a man of God? I feel hurt and somewhat frightened at the thought that my husband is acting out the same behaviors that both our fathers did. There is a saying that fruit doesn't fall far from the tree; and there are biblical references to children taking on the behavioral characteristics of parents. Is this a generational curse that will follow me and my family? I will not allow myself to be dragged through the mud like some women I know. I need to take a close look at what is going on in our life, and do something about it before things get totally out of hand.

Being married to the same man for fifteen years does not guarantee that our relationship is pure and Godly: was I living in a fantasy world all of this time? Did I make a mistake in marrying him and leaving him and our daughter for so many years? Questions, questions, I have so many questions that I need answers to! What am I going to say to him about last night? Do I just ignore it and move on as if it never happened?

It would disturb my peace and trust in him if I don't try to get an understanding of what is happening to us and our relationship. If he is drinking and smoking cigarettes, what else is he doing that breaks God's rules for his life, and our marriage? I have got to find out what's going on or our marriage will come to an end.

Ernest Lee and I have always been able to share our deepest thoughts, pain and disappointments with each other. What happened? I know that he is having problems on his job, but I don't believe that's the problem. Almost every weekend I hear him say that he feel's less than a man because he can't support his family the way he wants to. Maybe we should not have had so many children within such a short period of time. We are not like some people who see their children as a nuisance and an inconvenience rather than a blessing. Our children a burden, definitely not! They are a joy to us. However, with joy comes full responsibility for their care. God gives us everything we need to do what is necessary for them and ourselves. He is the Perfect Provider for all that we need. The fruit of my womb (our four children) is God's blessing to us. Frequently, especially during youth services at church, the preacher, and even my husband says that the family that has many children is a happy one. Well, today my family is not happy! Matter of fact I am very angry and I feel like letting it all out.

We both have jobs in the same company that does not treat us with the respect that we think we deserve: even though we work our jobs as unto the Lord. As believers, we expect some conflict on the job because we serve a different Lord than our boss, yet we expect respectful treatment there. An ideal world is not what we want; and we know that on this side of heaven we will live with tension we don't like. But each of us has gone through enough to know how to deal with racism, criticism, and discrimination in the workplace and everywhere else. This is why it baffles me that my husband, God's man, shows up at his home, in front of me and his children that he loves dearly, drunk and smelling like cigarettes. Is he doing his work on the job as unto the Lord? If he is, then how is Satan getting such an advantage in his life? He knows what my thoughts are, and what the Word says about drinking alcohol and smoking cigarettes. He preaches the same message every opportunity that he has. Apparently he is not the first partaker of the meal that he serves others–this is being hypocritical! Am I married to a hypocrite?

The Morning After . . .

Papa is still sleeping. He never sleeps through Saturday's breakfast; it is such a special time for all of us to be together as a family without being rushed. After we finish eating, Mama walks us kids over to Aunt Lucy Bell's apartment around the corner. I know why, and that makes me a little nervous. I wonder what is going to happen when Mama talks to Papa. She can really get upset sometimes, and when she does she cries a lot. I don't like seeing her cry; it makes me want to cry too.

When Mama returns to the apartment she goes directly into the bedroom. Her heart is beating fast and she is ready to hear an explanation for his bizarre behavior last night. "Ernest Lee, Ernest Lee, wake-up, we need to talk," she says. "What, what," he responds with eyes half open and thick speech as he sits up on the side of the bed. "What do you mean ?" "You know what I mean." "Honey, I don't know anything." "Well, let me refresh your memory. You came home late last night as drunk as a skunk with the smell of cigarettes all over you. You vomited all over the toilet; I had to clean you up, undress you and put you to bed. You have no idea of how upset the children were." "No I didn't, why are you telling these lies about me? You know what I think about drinking and smoking. Don't you?" "I thought I did; now I don't know anything. I don't even know if you are the man that I married! I will not live my life with a drunk who has no respect for himself or his family. And you call yourself a preacher of God's Word; you ought to be ashamed of yourself! Maybe you still have too much alcohol in your body to remember what you did. Why don't you go and wash up and I will heat up your breakfast." "I don't want any breakfast from a liar." "Ernest Lee Marcus, why don't you just go and take care of yourself in the bathroom. Something has come over you and I need to know what it is. Be sure of this one thing, I will find out everything that I need to know about everything." "What do you need to know?" "That is for you to tell me." "Okay, okay, I will tell you everything after I wash up and put my clothes on."

Ernest Lee is aware that the women in Mama's family are quick with the fist. They are known to physically abuse their boyfriends and husbands. He also remembers that she had a nervous breakdown and that he does not want to be responsible for triggering anything in her that may lead to a reoccurrence of that drama. He wants to be prepared to leave the apartment just in case that same fighting spirit is lying dormant in her, and is waiting to show itself strong against him.

END

Made in the USA
Lexington, KY
21 April 2011